# THE BOOK OF

# HOPES

# THE BOOK OF
# HOPES

Edited by
# KATHERINE
# RUNDELL

BLOOMSBURY
CHILDREN'S BOOKS
LONDON OXFORD NEW YORK NEW DELHI SYDNEY

*This book is dedicated to the doctors, nurses, carers, porters, cleaners and everyone currently working in hospitals: you are the stuff that wild, heroic tales are made of.*

# Contents

## More and More Animals

## True Stories

## Magic

## Crime and Detectives

## Playtime

## Amazing Machines

## Dragons, and Sea-Dragon Milk

## Books

## Do It Yourself

## Excellently Revolting

## Taking Flight

The Hope Tree by Axel Scheffler

# A very short note about hope

When the coronavirus pandemic began in the UK in 2020, I found myself urgently in need of hope. Because they are my greatest love, I went looking for it in books: old books, new books, terrifically serious books with footnotes in Latin and terrifically unserious books with jokes too rude to repeat here. And I found that, with each book I read, I felt just a little tougher: a little bolder, a little more ready to face the world.

And I think this is why: I think stories of transformation, of wild glories and everyday glories, of magic both real and imaginary, can act like a map. They give us a push towards hope. Real true hope isn't the promise that everything will be all right – but it's a belief that the world has so many strangenesses and possibilities that giving up would be a mistake; that we live in a universe shot through with the unexpected. There's never been a single decade in human history when we have not taken ourselves by surprise: we, the ungainly, wonky-toothed human species, have an endless potential for change. I am not an optimist, or a pessimist; I am a possibilityist. The possibilities out there for discovery, for knowledge, for transforming the world, are literally infinite – there are spectacular ideas that we will have in the next ten years that we can't even begin to dream of now.

So, during those first long months I began a Hope Project; I emailed some of the children's writers and artists whose work I love most. I asked them to write something very short, stories or facts, or draw something, anything, that would make the people reading it feel like possibilityists: something that would make them laugh or wonder or snort or smile. The response was magnificent, which shouldn't have surprised me, because children's writers and illustrators are professional hunters of hope. We seek it out, catching it in our nets, setting it down between the pages of a book, and sending it out into the world.

We put it online, to read for free, at the National Literacy Trust website, and the reception knocked me sideways. Schools made their own Books of Hopes; children sent me poems and stories and pictures and photographs of hope. It was a sudden and unexpected joy. Amid those hopes, my own is this: that this book (each copy of which raises money for NHS Charities Together) will be read long after the coronavirus pandemic has passed. I want it to be a book you can turn to whenever you find yourself in need of a shot of hope. It is, I think, a testament to what happens when you ask more than one hundred people to make something that will kick-start the engine of delight inside the human heart.

You could read this collection all in one sitting if you wanted to, but it's designed so that you can dip into it. There are true accounts of cats and hares and plastic-eating caterpillars, there are doodles and flowers, revolting poems and beautiful poems, there are stories of space travel and new shoes and elephants and dragons. None are longer than 500ish words, so they can be devoured in a bite: one story for breakfast and another at midday, with a poem, perhaps, for dessert.

*Katherine Rundell*
*July 2020*

# ANIMALS

# A Song of Gladness

by
## MICHAEL MORPURGO

I've been talking every morning to blackbird, telling him why we are all so sad at the moment. He sits on his branch and listens.

It was blackbird's idea. He sang out this morning at dawn from his treetop in the garden, to fox half-asleep behind the garden shed. She thought it a good idea too. It was a wake-up call. Fox was on her feet at once and trotting through Bluebell Wood, where she barked it to deer who ran off across the stream. Kingfisher was there, otter and dipper too. They heard and piped it on, and swallow swooped down over the meadow and passed it on to cows waiting to go into their milking, and to sheep resting quietly under the hedge with her lambs in the corner of the dew-damp field.

And they all agreed, bleating it out to bees already busy at their flowers, to weaving spiders, and grasshoppers, and scurrying mice. Trees heard sheep calling too, the whole flock of them, and waved their budding leaves in wild enthusiasm; and high above, the clouds wandered through the skies driven by wind, and wind took black-bird's idea over the cliffs across heaving seas, where gulls and albatross cried it out, and whales and dolphins and porpoises heard it, and wailed and whooped it down into the deep, where turtles listened, and they too loved the idea. So did plankton and every fish and crab and sea urchin and whelk, they all whispered that it was a fine notion, the best they ever heard. And the whisper went over the sea on the curling waves to the shores of Africa, where lions roared their approval, and elephants trumpeted it, leopards yawned it, water buffalo belched it, wild dogs yelped it. Wildebeest murmured it out across the savannah; and storm lifted the idea up over rainforests, where rain took it and poured it down on gorillas in the mist, on chimpanzees in their sleeping nests. Howler monkeys and gibbons echoed their calls loud over all the earth – they are that loud; and then from far up high, sun heard it too and shone it down over deserts where oryx stamped her foot, impatient to be getting on with it and doing it – she loved the idea that much. Even camel, who rarely joined in anything, thought this was the best and most beautiful idea he had ever heard.

Back in the garden, blackbird waited till everyone was ready. And then he began to sing. And the whole carnival of animals, every living thing on this good earth, joined in, until the globe echoed with the joy of it.

And blackbird was very pleased.

But I was still lost in sadness, as I heard the earth singing around me. It was a song of forgiveness. I knew that. So I asked blackbird if I could join in. And he sang his answer back to me.

'Why do you think we are doing this, you silly man? We want you and yours to be happy again. Only then will you treat us and the world right again, as you know you should. Only then will all be well. Sing, silly man, sing, sing. Our song is your song, your song is our song.'

So I sang, we all sang, sang away our sadness. In every house and flat and cottage, we clapped and sang, in every hut and tent, in every palace and hospital and prison. And they heard and we heard our song of gladness echoing all together, in glorious harmony across the universe.

# Care of Exotic Pets. Number 1. The Axolotl at Bedtime

by
## CATHERINE JOHNSON

Never give your axolotl chocolatl in a botl,
Serve it in a tiny eggcup, not too cold and not too hotl.
Make him sip it very slowly, not too much, never a lotl.
After all, he's just a sleepy, snuggly, bedtime axolotl.

Then tuck him – very gently – in his hand-carved wooden cotl.
Turn the light out, seven thirty, never later, on the dotl.
Sing him songs of salamanders, give it everything you've gotl,
As there's nothing like a tune to serenade your axolotl.

Brush his gills out on the pillow, never mind the whys or whatl.

Once he's deeply all a-slumber, sweetly snoring, off you trotl.

Think of him, snug in his dreamland, flying kites or sailing yachtl.

Then you'll sigh, you've done your duty, time to clean the pans
   and potl.

Come tomorrow he'll be one fresh, keen as mustard axolotl.

# The Monk and the Armadillo

by

## ONJALI Q. RAÚF

Situated somewhere between the cold, snowy peaks of Nepal and the tall, swaying mango trees of India, stands the highest mountain your imagination can possibly imagine. And right on the very top of this mountain's tip lay a single straw hut, inside which lived a monk – a very holy man, who believed it was his calling to sit on top of this mountain in complete isolation until he understood the depth and breadth of the universe, and everything in between.

Now, sitting in a straw hut all day and all night, with nothing but the sun and the moon and the wind to keep you company, can get awfully boring. Especially if you've been doing it for fifty years, as this very wise monk had. And so, deep down in his heart, the monk began to grow restless and started to hope for a sign. A sign that would tell him his knowledge was complete, that he had learned everything he could possibly learn, and that he should return back down the mountain to the beautiful village he had once grown up in, the friends he had left behind and the food he couldn't help dreaming about. Having survived on nothing but grains and seeds collected from between the rocks of the mountain for fifty years, the monk secretly hoped his sign would come soon. For oh! How he longed to taste a bowl of hot, delicious noodles, floating with a million spring onion hoops, just like his mother used to make. And even though he could have left the mountain at any time, the monk knew in his heart that he had to wait for a sign if he was to leave it in peace.

A year went by. And another. And another. And still the monk continued to secretly hope. Until one day, all the way from the golden, hot sands of Arabia, his sign began to make its way to him! For a mighty storm was hurtling across the desert plains and, like the inside of a giant washing machine, had snatched a poor armadillo up in its arms. The armadillo, frightened and alone, curled itself up into a tiny ball of iron armour and, squeezing its eyes tight, hoped with all its heart that it would land safe and sound and not too far from home. The storm was fierce and wild and hungry and, unknown to the arma-dillo, loved to travel. So imagine its surprise when, on feeling itself being dropped, the armadillo found itself not in a desert at all! But outside the door of a straw hut, situated on the snow-capped peak of a mountain that stood so high above the clouds it could almost touch the stars!

And imagine the monk's surprise when, just a few hours later, he opened his door to find a poor armadillo shaking at his feet.

'It is here!' cried the monk, lifting the armadillo up in his hands with a joyous smile. 'My sign is here! And it is in need of help!' And thanking the skies that had brought this little life to his door, the monk ran down the mountain at once to find help for his new friend.

I am pleased to say that the monk and the armadillo went on to become great friends, for each had fulfilled the hopes of the other. The monk by forever after keeping the armadillo warm and fed and happy, and the armadillo by inspiring the monk to become a vet and eat just as many bowls of hot, delicious noodles as he liked.

# Murkaster

by
## FRANK COTTRELL-BOYCE

You won't find Murkaster on a map. Maps show rivers, mountains and cities. They don't bother with clouds because clouds come and go.

Except in Murkaster.

The clouds came to Murkaster.

But they did not go away again.

They sat there on the roofs and in the squares and streets and gardens, until it was wiped off the map.

The world forgot Murkaster and Murkaster forgot the world.

If you were a Murkaster girl, like Sunny Hotspur for instance, you'd wear your hair in the Murkaster fashion – high and curly, like your own personal cloud. You'd shop or chat using Murkaster's special app, which was called Gloom. You would not go out, not without a mask and snorkel, because inside a cloud it's wet, dull and endless. Once, Sunny asked her mum, 'My name – Sunny – what does it even mean?'

'It's just one of those words that make you feel nice but don't actually mean anything.' There were a lot of words like that in the Murkaster dialect. For instance, 'view'.

There was a painting on the dining-room wall in the Hotspur house called *Foggy Day*. It showed a foggy day. There was another called *Cumulostratus* – which showed thick, grey clouds with streaks of golden yellow shining through the gaps. What were the streaks of yellow?

'It's because the painter ran out of grey and had to use that different colour,' said Mum.

Unconvinced, Sunny sat at her window scanning the passing murk for a glimpse of yellow.

She never saw the streak of yellow.

But she did see an eye – a deep, dark eye, set in a wrinkle of murk, staring at her. 'The murk,' reasoned Sunny, 'has an eye. So it must have a head. If it has a head, it must have a bottom. Which means the murk must have an end!'

Grabbing her mask and snorkel, she dashed outside. The moment she opened the door, she could hear something breathing. 'The murk has a voice,' she said to herself, and wondered if she could talk to it. That moment, something sniffed at her. Then, as if she was a flower, picked her up and hoisted her into the air.

You would have known right away that this was an elephant and that it was lifting her with its trunk. High into the damp air she rose until she was, yes, above the murk. The sky was blue. The distance was green. And sometimes blossom white. Above her head, streaks of yellow!

The elephant waved her around in the air. What was it doing? What did it want?

'You're lost!' yelled Sunny. 'You're lost in the murk, like us. You want me to find a way out?' She could guide the elephant out of here and leave the murk forever. But what about everyone else? Could she leave them all behind?

While she thought, the elephant blew impatiently and, where it breathed, the murk grew thinner and light showed through. And when it breathed, it sounded like a trumpet. And another trumpet answered and another and another. There must be a dozen elephants lost in the murk.

Sunny swung the trunk this way and that, steering her elephant towards the nearest elephant, then leading the two to the next elephant and the next until she brought a dozen elephants together in the centre of the murk. 'Now sing!' she cried. 'Sing me a city.'

And a dozen elephants trumpeted their happiness at finding each other and their trumpeting tore the murk apart like tissue paper and unwrapped a city – with domes and towers and bridges and minarets and waterways – the city Sunny had lived in but never till that moment seen.

# Hope
by
**Tom Percival**

# HOPE IN UNEXPECTED PLACES

# Hope

by
## ANTHONY HOROWITZ

The town of Hope, near Aberdeen
Is somewhere I have seldom been
But then it's not a tourist trap –
It isn't even on the map!

There's certainly not much to see
They've closed the local library
Because they said there is no need
When no one in the town can read
They've got a pub and a hotel
But neither of them's doing well
The hotel isn't quite the Ritz
The beds have fleas, the staff have nits
The only pub, 'The Rose and Crown',
Is easily the worst in town.

The one theatre's sadly gone
It burned down while a play was on

(The critics thought the play so dire
That all of them preferred the fire.)
The cinema is second rate
The films are always out of date
The last James Bond film that I saw
Had Bond still played by Roger Moore.


The pavements are never clean
Because the council's far too mean
To pay for cleaners – and the park
Is only open after dark
The grass is lumpy, full of weeds
And dogs can only walk on leads
There is a children's playground but
When school is finished, it is shut.


The Chief of Police is eighty-two
He can't catch crooks. He can't catch flu!
The vicar surely won't be missed
Since he's become an atheist
The mayor sold his golden chain
And then was never seen again
The local paper isn't bought
Because there's nothing to report.
The school is like a concrete bunker
Matron's drunk. The head is drunker.

Now, living here must really stink
At least, that is what you might think
But that is simply not the case
There is no more delightful place
The fun and laughter never ends
Everyone is best of friends.
And all the residents agree
There's nowhere else they'd rather be.

So if you're feeling uninspired,
Sleeping badly, waking tired
If everything is going wrong,
The day feels dark, the night's too long
Remember all the people who
Have found the following is true:

**It's so much easier to cope**
**If you decide to live in Hope.**

# An extract from
# *The Knife of Never Letting Go*

by
## PATRICK NESS

'But there's always hope,' Ben says. 'You always have to hope.'

We both look at him and there must be a word for how we're doing it but I don't know what that is. We're looking at him like he's speaking a foreign language, like he just said he was moving to one of the moons, like he's telling us it's all just been a bad dream and there's candy for everybody.

'There ain't a whole lotta hope out here, Ben,' I say.

He shakes his head. 'What d'you think's been driving you on? What d'you think's got you this far?'

'Fear,' Viola says.

'Desperayshun,' I say.

'No,' he says, taking us both in. 'No, no, no. You've come farther than most people on this planet will do in their lifetimes. You've over-come obstacles and dangers and things that should've killed you. You've outrun an army and a madman and a deadly illness and seen things most people will never see. How do you think you could have possibly come that far if you didn't have hope?'

Viola and I exchange a glance.

'I see what yer trying to say, Ben—' I start.

'Hope,' he says, squeezing my arm on the word. 'It's hope. I'm look-ing into yer eyes right now and I am telling you that there's hope for you, hope for you both.' He looks up at Viola and back at me. 'There's hope waiting for you at the end of the road.'

# Mr Umbo's Umbrellas

by
## PATIENCE AGBABI

Three months, we've been underground,
hunched in fleeces, fake furs,
waiting for the sign

to change on the Southbound
via Bank, Westbound to Harrow-on-the-Hill;
while Mr Umbo,

fresh from Cameroon
via the Paris Metro,
breeds in his squat portmanteau

a culture of umbrellas,
yellowing, each one in its
pale-cream sleeve.

*It never rains*
*but it shines,*
he sings into the gloom.

We wait in mohair, moleskin,
each parasol-parapluie
a gift that will open

on the flicker of neon,
the crackle of announcement
that Spring is in the air.

When it comes,
we hold each quivering cocoon
up up up into the light

Spring rain; and, from ruched skin,
the umbrellas
emerge:

spider-ribbed, spike-tipped, they flap
upwards, outwards, to resplendent
domes of yellow yellow

at Bank, Hill, Park, Green,
Wood, Valley, Common, Garden:
all over London

Mr Umbo's Umbrellas,
yellow as the rain's grey,
spring into bloom.

# Bag for Life

by

## JOSEPH ELLIOTT

'What's in the bag?' I ask for the umpteenth time.

*Umpteenth* ... Such a weird word. Ump-teenth, ump-teeth. The image of what an ump monster might look like appears in my head, complete with row upon row of garish teeth. It's funny how your mind occupies itself when you've got nothing to do but walk. I push aside a low-hanging branch so it doesn't thwack me in the face.

'You'll find out soon, Amila,' says Dad. His answers are always vague when I ask about the bag. 'I'm saving it for when we really need it.' He's told me that before.

Dad's been clutching the bag ever since we entered the forest. I'm not sure where or when he picked it up. It's the only thing either of us are holding; we left too quickly to take anything else. The bag is from a supermarket – it's one of those 'bag for life' ones. It's orange and the writing on it is cracked and faded. The plastic's too thick to see through. Trust me, I've tried.

There's food inside, I know that much. It has to be food. Dad says we have to save it for when we're desperate, but I don't know how much more desperate we need to be. We've been walking for two days already and all I've eaten is a handful of blackberries and some wild mushrooms, which made my stomach cramp.

From the look of its weight and the way the bag swings, I think it's tins. Maybe tuna or baked beans or spaghetti hoops. Spaghetti hoops are my favourite. On toast, with loads of butter. My mouth starts salivating at the thought of it.

Or perhaps it's dog food. Right now, I'm so hungry I'd even eat that. I'd probably enjoy it too.

'Can we eat the food yet?'

'No.'

'What about now?'

'No.'

'What about now?'

'No.'

That's about the extent of our conversations in the days that follow. My feet are sore, my back aches, my whole body feels like it's falling apart. We're never getting out of here.

I keep my eyes on the bag for life as it sways back and forth, back and forth. Maybe it's not tins. Maybe it's chocolate or biscuits or—

'Look!' says Dad. 'Over there.' There's a massive grin on his face.

I was so lost in my thoughts, I hadn't even noticed we'd left the forest. I follow Dad's finger and see the buildings. There's smoke coming out of the chimneys.

'People!' I say.

'We're going to be all right,' says Dad.

'But what about the food? …' I point at the bag. 'We never ate it.'

'No,' says Dad. 'We didn't.'

Then he does what I've been wanting him to do ever since we entered the forest; he opens the bag.

I hold my breath and peer inside.

'Oh,' I say, and then I understand.

At the bottom of the bag, smooth and grey and speckled with dirt, are three large stones.

# The Hope Hunters
by
## Axel Scheffler

# THE STARS

Stargazing by Emily Fox

# A Way to the Stars

by
## DAVID ALMOND

Let's make a picture book together. Here are the words.
Now do the pictures. Or just imagine the pictures.
Or have a sleep and dream the pictures.

The boy wanted to find a way to the stars.
His pals just laughed.
In your dreams! They said.
But his dad said he would help.
They had some food.
They had a think.
They made a ladder.
Up they went.
Whoops!
They built a tower.
Up they went.
Crash!
They built a rocket.

Up they went.

Nope!

And then a trampoline. A pair of wings. A pogo stick. A cannon!

Up! Up! Up! Up!

No! No! No! No!

Hahahahahahaha!

What a mess! What a laugh!

They had some food.

They had a think.

They built a shed.

So beautiful.

They went inside.

So very dark.

They painted moons. They painted stars. They painted galaxies.

So very beautiful and bright.

They fell asleep.

They had their dreams.

Astonishing!

Astonishing!

Up! Up! Up! Up!

Yes! Yes! Yes! Yes!

Only in the darkness can you see the stars.

Martin Luther King Jr

Only in the Darkness Can You See the Stars
by Lydia Monks

# KINDNESSES

# Say Something Nice

by
## A.F. HARROLD

Every now and then
say something nice.

Say it to a friend.

Say it to a teacher.

Say it to your sister
or brother,
your father or mother.

Say something nice like:

*You remind me of flowers.*

or

*Your hair is like fresh bread.*

or

*I like sausages.*

or

*You're better than asparagus.*

or

*I like you more than Simon.*

Just say something nice
to make them feel good.

The world is sometimes grey
and things go wrong
but a kind word,
and a smile,
can turn it back around.

Say something nice like:

*That wasn't a very good poem
but I liked it when it stopped.*

# New Boots

by
## JACQUELINE WILSON

There's a huge hole in my right boot and the sole flaps madly on my left. Our Lily used to pass down her boots to me, but now my feet have grown too big, even though she's much older than me. She's away in service, working as a lady's maid.

*I* don't want to be a lady's maid. I want to be the lady! My teacher says I've got a chance of getting a scholarship to the Girls' High School next year. I go past it when I go to Biggerton market on errands for Ma. I can't see me fitting in with all those posh girls in their fancy uniform, to be honest. Mind you, I don't really fit in at the village school either.

They all call me Spud. It is not my real name, obviously. Ma gave us girls flowery names. I'm Rose, and my older sisters are Lily and Violet. I'm called Spud because of my brown frock. Ma made it out of cheap material and it's so coarse it sets me itching something chronic. The children at school say it's made out of old potato sacking. Hence, Spud.

If I ever get to be a lady, I shall wear silk frocks all the shades of the rainbow. Though a queen is the highest lady in the land and poor old Victoria wears nothing but black every day.

There's a wonderful evening gown in the draper's shop window in Biggerton. It's a rich Prussian blue, with red satin trimmings and red cut-glass beads on the bodice. Someone has arranged a pair of scarlet kid boots beside the deep blue hem, the perfect touch.

I am here to buy flour and cheese and a dozen eggs because our old Henny Penny's stopped laying, but now I have the groceries I must have one more look at the dazzling gown.

But when I glimpse the draper's window, the dress is missing! Has someone purchased my beautiful gown? I rush to see, and the sole on my left boot catches on a pebble. I stagger and land on my knees, juggling flour and cheese and eggs.

The lady from the draper's shop dashes out and picks me up.

I burst into tears and then duck my head, ashamed.

'Don't cry, child! You've saved every single egg! But, oh dear, look at the state of your boots!' she says.

The sole has torn right off, and my bare foot is touching the ground now.

'Are these your only pair?' she asks gently, and I nod.

'We don't really stock children's boots. The only footwear I have in my shop are scarlet boots to go with an evening gown, but the lady who bought it didn't care for the ensemble. They're ridiculously fancy and probably far too big for you, but you're welcome to try them,' she says.

They're a perfect fit for my big feet! The kid feels soft as a glove, but the sole is stout.

'They're the most beautiful boots in all the world – but I couldn't possibly afford them,' I say, sniffing.

The lady looks at me. She looks at the boots.

'Take them, dear,' she says. 'When you start earning you can come and pay me. How about that?'

Oh joy! When I am a lady, I shall buy *all* my gowns and boots from her! And though I'm still an ungainly girl in a brown dress, I feel like a queen. I dance all the way home in my new boots, my beautiful, red kid boots!

# Searching for Treasure

by
## ANNABEL PITCHER

Alex lay on his bedroom carpet and sighed. It was that kind of day. The world was exhaling thick, grey breath and the birds' lungs were filled with lead. Even the flowers seemed unable to lift their heads, or so Alex imagined. He couldn't be bothered to lift his own head to peer out of the window and look at the garden.

It was that kind of day. Again.

Rolling on to his stomach, Alex shut his eyes and buried his face in his blue, fluffy rug. His door flew open. 'Quick! Quick! There's a—' a voice started, and then stopped. 'What are you doing?'

'Go away, George,' Alex said. George, his younger brother, entered the room instead. 'I'm sleeping.'

'Liar.'

Alex opened one eye. 'What are *you* doing? Apart from annoying me.'

George grinned. He performed a spin in his bright green wellies, then tucked his thumbs beneath the shoulder straps of his dinosaur rucksack. 'We're going on an adventure. Like we used to.'

Alex shook his head. 'Nah. You're all right.'

'But didn't you see it?' George asked.

'See what?'

George hopped over Alex's legs, then dashed to the window. 'The rainbow, of course!'

Alex crawled after him, grabbed hold of the radiator and pulled himself up. 'There's nothing but fog, mate.'

'*Above* the fog,' George replied. 'You need my special binoculars.' He made a pair out of his hands and held them to Alex's face. 'See it?'

Alex was about to say no. He always said no lately, but his brother's hands were small and clammy with excitement. 'Oh yeah,' he said, pretending to adjust the focus by twiddling George's little finger. It moved something inside him as well. 'You're right.'

George dropped to his knees. 'I plotted it on a map!' he said, rooting through his rucksack. 'Here.' He held up a page torn from an atlas. 'The pot of gold is in …' His eyes shone as he pointed at the town he'd circled in pink felt-tip pen. '… *Blackpool*.'

'Hmm,' Alex said. 'That's quite a distance. Do you mean Blackpool, or do you mean *black pool*? The pond down the road is sort of black. And it's a pool of water. Should we try there first?'

'Yeah,' George said. 'Yeah, OK!' He stuffed the map back into his rucksack, then paused. 'Are you actually coming? Actually actually?'

'You need some help finding this gold, right?'

'Yeah,' George said, but he didn't move. He was staring out of the window. The mist had thinned to reveal a nondescript sky. 'But what if there isn't really a rainbow?' he asked, his fingers and face all in a knot. 'I can't really see one.'

'Can't you?' Alex replied. He made some binoculars out of his own hands, then held them up to his brother's face. Somewhere out-side, a bird burst into song or perhaps it had been singing all along. Flowers lifted their heads towards a sky, a day, a world filling with colour. 'I can.'

# Balcony Picnic

by
## MICHELLE MAGORIAN

Up on the balcony, high in the air
Drinking fizzy orange in an old deck chair,
The washing hangs above me, the traffic's far below,
And Mum is carrying sandwiches, but on tiptoe.

My little sister's sleeping so it's just Mum and me,
And we're having chocolate fingers for our picnic tea,
And sandwiches with jam, buns and sausage rolls,
And ice cream and jelly in yellow plastic bowls.

We mustn't laugh too loud in case my sister wakes,
So we're whispering very quietly, and eating fairy cakes.
Nobody can see us watching planes fly by,
Sitting here and eating our picnic in the sky.

# A Big Hug

by

## Catherine Rayner

# DREAMING AND DAYDREAMING

Hopes and Dreams by Yasmeen Ismail

# Look Out
## A Poem of Hope

by
### PHILIP ARDAGH

Look out of your window.
What do you see?
Do you see what I see?
Do you see the savannah?
The tundra?
An endless sea of sand
Or sheets of ice?
Do you see sky meeting
Land
Like two brushstrokes
One of blue
And one of green?
Do you see
Wide open spaces
From your tiny box;

Endless possibilities
Of footsteps
Yet to be trodden,
Air yet to be breathed,
And oceans crossed?
You do?
I do, too.
For this is hope
And hope becomes
Reality
When the window
Becomes a door
And you can throw it wide.

Perchance to Dream by Chris Riddell

# DOGS

Plumdog Delight by Emma Chichester Clark

# Daphne and the Doughnuts

by

## JESSIE BURTON

Daphne (an old-fashioned name, pronounced *Daffknee*) was a very sensible girl. She ate the crusts off her toast, not just the butter-drenched bits in the middle. She made her bed in the morning, and at night she felt like a letter slipping into a fresh envelope, posting herself to pleasant dreams. She always unlaced her shoes before taking them off. She knew that the sky was blue. She would say to me, 'Jessie, you know that ghosts aren't real, don't you?' (I had, I will admit, suggested otherwise.) And even though Daphne read stories in which animals talked – monkeys, tigers, lions, parrots, cats, bears, you name it, chattering away! – she would declare to me that in real life this was absolutely, categorically *impossible*.

One sunny day, Daphne was walking home with her mother through the park, her shoes done up tightly, of course: no laces trailing anywhere to trip her up. They had visited the bakery, and Daphne was carrying a box of jam doughnuts. She hadn't even asked if she could have a bite before dinner. That's how sensible Daphne was.

When they stopped at the pond to look at the ducks, a very small Yorkshire terrier trotted up and sat by Daphne's feet. Daphne continued to watch the ducks.

'Gizza doughnut,' said a voice.

Daphne looked around. It sounded like an old man, croaky yet hungry. Where was this old man, his gnarled fingers reaching for her delicious treats?

'Oi,' said the voice again. 'Down 'ere. Gizza doughnut. I'm *starvin'*.'

Daphne peered down. The little dog was sitting expectantly on his haunches, and her words were in the air before she could stop them. 'They're for after dinner,' she whispered. *That's it*, she thought. *I've gone crazy. I'm talking to a dog.*

'Just one,' the dog whispered back, his beady eyes imploring. 'I bet you've got at least six.'

Daphne blinked. He was right: she had six doughnuts in this box. She looked towards her mum, who was making an appointment on her phone to the family dentist.

'You 'ave one too,' the dog wheezed. 'That'll make it fun.'

He really wanted a doughnut. He really wanted Daphne to have a doughnut. Daphne opened the box and dropped one by his tiny paws. He snatched it, jam squirting and sugar sprinkling everywhere. Daphne closed her eyes and took one in her jaws, too. She stood in the sun with the little dog, scoffing a doughnut BEFORE DINNER. Oh, it was delicious! So perfect, so sweet and warm and soft! Never, in the long history of doughnuts, had a doughnut tasted better!

When she opened her eyes, the dog had disappeared. Daphne checked: four doughnuts left. He had been a very persuasive dog. It felt like the sun was setting in her stomach. As her mother ended her call to the dentist, Daphne licked the last grains of sugar off her fingers, glinting like diamonds in the light.

As I said: Daphne was a very sensible girl.

# A Dog in Time

## by
## LAUREN ST JOHN

Before he moved out, Ellie's dad was her human alarm clock.

'Ready? Steady? GO!' he'd cry as he burst into her room each morning.

Heart pounding, Ellie would bolt upright – often from a dead sleep. From that moment on, her entire family ran at life as if it were an Olympic event.

Suitcases in the hall meant that Dad was jet-setting off on a business trip. He'd dash out to the taxi as Ellie and her mum rushed about getting ready, clutching half-eaten bits of toast. Their nerves jangled if the traffic held them up. Her mum had to catch a train.

School was a whirl too. The bell jangled constantly. Exam preparation, activities, extra lessons, more exams.

Ellie's head span. Back home, pizza stiffened and gravy congealed as homework and pinging messages swallowed dinner time. Her dad was always missing. Her mum's hugs were distracted.

Ellie's dreams were filled with dogs. Plump golden Labrador pups, whip-smart Border collies, mongrels with soulful eyes. To Ellie, dogs equalled love.

'We don't have time for a dog!' her parents would chorus, snatching out their phones to check emails and news headlines.

*They did have time to get divorced*, Ellie thought bitterly now, as the school bell rang. Children exploded out the gates. Ellie ran too. She had a mountain of homework. Her mum was in such a hurry to get home, she took a shortcut. And got a puncture.

As her mum fretted about the tyre and her work deadline, Ellie spotted a crawling bee by the side of the country lane.

'It needs some sugar water if it's to survive,' said her mum. Tyre forgotten, she mixed a little from a flask and sugar sachet. She laughed with delight when the bee revived and flew away. It was the first time she'd laughed in weeks.

Ellie exhaled. 'Listen to the birdsong.'

'And the breeze in the leaves,' smiled her mum. 'Wait, what was that?'

They both heard it: a faint whine. A path led to a field, where they found a thin, fearful stray dog caught in a rabbit snare. Ellie's mum bound its paw with a torn strip of shirt. Ellie soothed it while her mother changed the tyre before driving them to the vet.

'What about your deadline?' asked Ellie.

'Nothing matters more than saving a life.'

Lucky, as they named the dog, moved in and saved them right back. At weekends, they breathed in pine forests, hiked hills, and lay in meadows of poppies and cornflowers.

Television was a thing of the past. Ellie's mother quit her job and freelanced from home. She discovered talents for gardening and cooking. Every day, she and Lucky enjoyed walking Ellie to and from school.

Ellie fell in love with painting – and Lucky.

Dogs slow life down. When they look at you, they really look at you and their soulful eyes ask that you see them too.

'Mind if we take a detour to watch the sun go down over the river?' Ellie would often ask her mum as they walked home. 'Do we have time?'

'All the time in the world.'

# The Toilet Ghost Dog!

by
## PAMELA BUTCHART

One time, we got locked in the toilets after school when we'd been having an EMERGENCY MEETING about how the shepherd's pie at school dinners was getting WORSE and how we needed to speak to the POLICE or maybe even the ARMY about it because the dinner ladies wouldn't stop making it and they needed to be STOPPED.

But then we heard a noise and Jodi said, 'SHHHHHH!' because we weren't supposed to be there and Zach DEFINITELY wasn't supposed to be there because we were in the GIRLS' TOILETS and we'd basically had to DRAG him in.

But then we heard a KEY turn and I GASPED and Zach said, 'That's not good.' And it WASN'T because we'd just been LOCKED IN.

Maisie started to PANIC but then Jodi said it was OK because we could drink water from the TAPS so we wouldn't die of THIRST but that we needed FOOD.

So Maisie handed her a custard cream and Jodi started cutting it into TINY pieces with her ruler so we wouldn't STARVE.

But then suddenly there was SCRATCHING at the door and Zach yelled, 'HELP! WE'RE TRAPPED!'

And that's when Jodi dropped the ruler and put her hand over Zach's mouth and whispered, 'That's not a teacher. Teachers don't scratch!'

Then we heard SNUFFLING and I looked at Jodi and she looked at me because we KNEW what was OUTSIDE because we'd heard the RUMOURS.

But then Maisie said, 'WHAT?!'

So I took a deep breath and said, 'It's the GHOST HOUND.'

And Maisie's eyes went SWIRLY and she fainted. Because even though LOADS of weird stuff has happened at our school, like the time with the BABY ALIENS and the WEREWOLF and the DEMON DINNER LADIES, this was different because this was a BEAST who was also a GHOST.

That's when Zach spotted a window and said we should try to squeeze through it, but Jodi said the GHOST HOUND would FOLLOW US.

Jodi said that if we WHISTLED really loudly the ghost hound might run away because dogs HATE high-pitched sounds.

So we CREPT up to the door and waited for Jodi to give us the SIGNAL and then we whistled as LOUDLY as we could.

But then the ghost hound started HOWLING. And it howled so loudly, it woke Maisie and she SCREAMED.

And even though it was TOTAL CHAOS, that's when I had an idea. I looked at Jodi and said, 'Hand me the custard cream.'

And then I threw it on the ground and Zach GASPED, but I said, 'Trust me.'

Then I kicked it under the door and the hound stopped howling and started MUNCHING.

And I yelled, 'GO! GO! GO!' and climbed out the window.

But then, once we were outside, we heard WHIMPERING and Maisie said, 'I don't think it's a ghost hound. It's a GHOST DOG. And it's sad!'

And before we could stop her, Maisie RAN, so we ran after her and that's when we GASPED, because it WASN'T a GHOST HOUND.

It was the TINIEST PUPPY EVER and it had biscuit crumbs all over its face!

We took the puppy home and Jodi's mum phoned the number on its collar and an old man came and he was CRYING because he'd lost the puppy DAYS ago.

The man thanked us loads and said, 'Time to go home, Cuddles!'

And we burst out laughing because we couldn't believe we'd been scared of a puppy called CUDDLES!

But then suddenly Maisie stopped laughing and said, 'Wait. That means there's still a GHOST HOUND loose in our school? Doesn't it? DOESN'T IT?!'

Mouse by **Emily Sutton**

# CATS

# Be More Cat

by
## KIRAN MILLWOOD HARGRAVE

When I want to feel really happy, I think like my cat. My cat leads, what might appear to be, a very simple life to you or me. But really she leads the most exciting, dangerous and contented existence anyone could imagine.

Where you or I see a sliver of sunlight cutting across the carpet, she sees a warm cloud perfect for sleeping. Where you or I see a pile of laundry ready to be put in the machine, she sees a cushiony cloud perfect for sleeping. Where you or I see a newspaper, she sees a crinkly cloud perfect for sleeping.

But it is not all about sleeping. The life of a cat is fraught with responsibility.

Where you or I see that same pile of laundry now hung out to dry on the line, she sees ghosts and must use all her skill in claw-climbing to slay them. Where you or I see a box, she sees uncharted territory to be explored, conquered and sat in. Where you or I see the friendly neighbourhood stray, she sees a tiger who must be hissed at and chased, tail made fluffy as a raccoon's. Where you or I see geese, flying in their perfect V high in the sky, my tiny white-and-black cat sees dinner and leaps with all her might.

So live your life with the self-belief of a tiny black-and-white cat, leaping with the conviction that she can swat birds from the sky, slay ghosts and scare away tigers. Imagine a world where a house is a kingdom, a box a throne. Take love wherever you can find it, move to find the last warm parts of the day, spend hours excited by a leaf (but maybe don't try the bum-licking).

So my new motto is: be more cat. And remember, if ever the adventures become too much, there's always a cloud, crinkly, warm and cushiony, waiting.

# Hold on to Hope by Katie Abey

All tough times end and you will get through every challenge that comes your way, just like you always have before. Hold on to hope.

# The Naughtiest Cat
# I Have Ever Known

by
## SF SAID

I was an only child. I grew up in a flat with a single mum, alone. I had friends at school, but life at home was quiet, solitary, isolated. All this changed when I was eleven, because that was when we got a cat: the naughtiest cat I've ever known.

He was a tiny kitten when we first met him, just a few weeks old. He was so small, he could sit in the palm of your hand. His fur was entirely black, except for a single fleck of white on his chest. I called him Monamy. The name comes from French. It means 'my friend' – 'mon ami'. That seemed the perfect name for this kitten, who soon became more than a friend to me. He was like a brother: the best little brother I could imagine.

We lived in a third-floor flat, so Monamy had to be an indoor cat. He soon tore our furniture to shreds. And our carpets. And our curtains. He loved to climb those curtains. He would swarm up them to the very top, as if they were trees, and sit there proudly surveying his domain. Or he'd swing wildly back and forth on them, until my mum shouted him down.

I have to admit, I encouraged him. We both had a lot of energy to let out, being stuck indoors. So we played endless games together: hunting, chasing, even football and rugby. He was a great tackler, very ferocious, and a great fighter too. Ambush attacks were his favourite. He loved to spring out at you and maul your legs. I still have a scar that dates back to that time! But I didn't mind a bit.

Monamy's greatest moment came one night when we had an unwanted guest who we were forced to see because she was a relative. She was very self-important and made it very clear that she hated cats. For most of the evening, Monamy left her alone ... but he was just waiting for his moment.

Deep in the shadows behind her, out of everyone's view but mine, he found the perfect position – and then leaped like a great black panther, swooping straight up and over her head. She shrieked as she saw the panther flying through the air. But he didn't touch her. He sailed right over her and landed gracefully on the other side. Then he turned, gave her a look as if to say, 'How about that, then?' and walked off calmly, his tail held high. Our guest left shortly afterwards. I thought that was the most amazing thing I'd ever seen.

It's been years and years, but I still think about him. He made a massive impact on my life, helping me through some hard times. My memories of him definitely played a part in the writing of *Varjak Paw*. In fact, I remember writing stories about him at the time. So maybe it was inevitable that my first book would be about a cat!

# Lockdown Cat Haircut

by
## SHARON DAVEY

**Elle**

Don't be afraid, dear.
Just sit in this chair.
I'm going to give you
Superb lockdown hair.

Let's look at your face.
The shade of your eyes.
D'you want a bowl cut?
Or sparkly surprise?

Good choice to come to
Elle's hair place today.
I'll make you a rainbow
And wash out the grey.

Friends will all love it!
I promise you that.

It's fine! It's OK
That you're next door's cat!

**Cat**

I guess she'll be great
At haircuts and bows?
Though six is quite young –
Oh gosh. Well, here goes!

She's doing it now!
She's snipping my hair.
It won best in show
At the local spring fair.

'Excuse me, my dear,
I really can't stay.
I can smell dinner.
Nooo! Please not hairspray!'

# The Meeting

by
## NIZRANA FAROOK

A pitiful mewl made Salma stop on the path to the village and prick up her ears.

She stretched up on her toes and looked over the wild shrubbery. Giant purple jungle flowers swayed in the sunshine. There was that sound again. There was something ... *pleading* about it.

Parting velvety leaves that left a yellow powder on her fingers, Salma hurried towards what sounded like a kitten in pain. There was a woody smell of dried mud and, among a thicket of trees, a hole in the ground.

She peered into the hole and drew back in fright, scrambling away. It was a cat all right, but not the type she was expecting.

Salma stopped mid-flight. *Why* had the animal been so still?

She crept back towards the hole.

The leopard looked weak and spent, as if it had been trying to escape for a while. Salma watched its orange specks, circled in mottled black, as they rose and fell.

What was wrong with it? Normally they could jump great heights.

She crouched down at the lip of the hole and looked closely. One leg was bloody, possibly at the knee.

So that was why it couldn't jump.

She should go and get help. But the leopard was too close to the village – some people might want to kill it in case it attacked someone.

But if it stayed here, it would die.

She really should leave it and go home. It was injured. It would possibly die anyway.

But it was young, probably not long separated from its mother, with its whole life ahead. If it got out, it would have a fighting chance of survival. Maybe there was some hope its leg would heal and it would live and hunt as normal again.

Salma quickly got looking for a suitable branch. She dragged it into the hole, with the top sticking up outside.

The leopard gripped the end of the branch and shimmied its way up, dragging its injured leg behind. It sprang out in front of Salma, making her recoil into the broad trunk of an atamba tree.

She pressed against the tree, shaking. She hadn't expected it to be so quick.

She'd *helped* it. Why would it do this?

The leopard stared into her eyes. What was it that you were supposed to do? Look them in the eye or *don't* look them in the eye? It was hard to remember when you had a big cat standing in front of you, hungry for its next meal.

Its eyes were wise, almost humanlike, turned up at the ends as if penciled in kohl. It smelt of sweat and wet cat, only stronger.

It narrowed its eyes and, just like that, Salma was sure it meant her no harm. The eyes seemed to be telling her something, she didn't know what. It held her gaze for a moment and walked away, flicking its tail in farewell.

Salma shivered. She would never forget this day, this leopard, this meeting.

# BIRDS

# Hope; or, Learning the Language of Birds

by
## JACKIE MORRIS

In years to come you would think of this time as the 'time of the
　　great quiet'.
It would seem to you, then, that the earth was holding her breath.
Waiting.
Watching.
Cars silent in the streets.
Planes absent from the sky.

After a week the air would seem cleaner, colours brighter.

But the nights seemed darker, perhaps because the stars glowed
　　brighter.
Fear wandered the dreams of some. Anxiety stalked.
And you would wake in early morning, as the light slipped into
　　each day,
and listen.

You would hear sweet notes rising with the sun, to greet the light.
You would hear, across the silence, a response.
You would listen, as other voices lifted to song.
You would begin to learn each different voice, begin to see them.
And soon they were no longer just 'birds' but became wren, robin,
blackbird, thrush, greenfinch, goldfinch, sparrow, jay.
And you would follow the textures of birdsong, call and response,
as it moved with the sun.
And you would feel for the first time how the sun was lifted into the
sky each day,
on birdsong.
You would feel the turning of the earth beneath your feet,
as the song travelled with the path of the light.
You would hear the turning of the world
as each day dawns,
at the edge of the darkness,
at the edge of the light.
You would know that others were listening
as the song moved with the light.

And you would learn that, if for a while it seemed the earth stood
still,
holding her breath,
if it seemed that the nights were darker,
somewhere on the turning world the sun was rising,
the birds were singing,
a wave of song in an ocean of sky.

And you would know
that others too would hear those voices.

Out of the silence,
just before dawn,
you would find the threads of hope
as the breath of birds became song.

# The Lamagaia Nest

by
## JASBINDER BILAN

*This is an extra-special scene inspired by my debut* Asha and the Spirit Bird *– I hope you enjoy reading it as much as I loved writing it.*

I grasp Nanijee's hand tight as we scramble together over loose stones and winding steep paths. We're heading through the snow-capped Himalaya, to a special place that Nanijee has been promising to show me, a place where the wide-winged lamagaias nest.

The sky, like a never-ending blue ribbon, stretches ahead of us, leading us higher, further until my legs ache. We rest by a cold stream bubbling between two hefty boulders and scoop iced water with our cupped palms.

'Is it much further?' I flop on to the grassy slope and spot a bird of prey spiralling close to the jagged snowy peaks above us.

'No, Asha dear, not far now.' Nanijee unknots a white cotton bundle and hands me a round pastry sprinkled with tiny nibs of *ajwain*. 'Eat this as we go, it will help.'

I munch the crisp pastry as we follow the high-pitched cries of the circling lamagaias, climbing until we reach a wide plateau where tufts of wild grasses whisper among midnight-blue poppies.

'Shush,' says Nanijee, resting a finger on her lips. 'We must stay quiet if we want to see them.'

I trail behind her, treading softly, the hot flame of hope firing in my chest. Nanijee leads me to a flat ledge and we crouch low, peering over the dizzying side at the dots of grey houses below and the shimmering, dancing lake.

I clutch Nanijee's hand tighter and follow her gaze where I almost can't look for the snap of excitement pulling at my insides.

'See?'

Staying as still as I can, my eyes find the nook, tucked close to the sheer rock, where a nest of sticks and straw holds the treasure we've been searching for.

Two soft fluffy chicks, their white feathers like the softest cotton wool, snuggle together. Coal-black eyes stare into the distance, ravenous for food.

Nanijee flicks me a smile. 'I told you we'd find them.'

A whoosh of air and bronze wings arrive in a whirlwind below us and nudge into the nook; the lamagaias have come to feed their babies. Gripping the rock with sharp silver claws, they drop chunks of fresh meat into the chicks' gaping beaks.

We shuffle closer together, watching the lamagaias feed, admiring the majestic birds with their smooth feathered wings, rippling dark over golden.

'They're beautiful,' I whisper. 'Thank you for bringing me all this way to see them.'

'I've always loved lamagaias,' says Nanijee. 'I don't know why ... Maybe they remind me of when I was a girl like you and used to look after our goats. I'd see the lamagaias swooping and circling, putting on such a show.'

Nanijee squeezes my hand and we move away from the drop, watch the birds of prey spread their immense wings with a shudder and leave their chicks to go hunting again.

She threads an arm around my shoulder. 'Imagine if *we* could fly like that!'

'I love you, Nanijee.'

'I'll always stay with you, Asha.'

# Vince

by
## SARAH CROSSAN

Once upon a time there was an ugly duckling
with grey frayed feathers
who made sounds so awful and so often
that everyone else living around the pond
asked Alexa to yank up the volume on their speakers
so Stormzy could drown out the squawk
of poor old Vince trying to sing.

Yes, Vince was *very* ugly indeed
but his brothers and sisters
loved him all the same
because sometimes siblings can be kind like that.
And yes, Vince was a *terrible* singer,
but his mother and father believed he was perfect
because parents often feel that way
even about their noisiest ducklings.

So Vince grew up and stayed just as he was, mostly,
turning into a very ugly drake.
But he didn't care because many things
mattered more than what he wore.

Vince was the smartest of the flock
who studied medicine over at the big lake
and when he returned swinging his stethoscope
and mending broken wings,
everyone called him a quacking hero.

Because that's exactly what Vince was.

# INSECTS
# AND BUGS

Beastie Besties by **Sara Ogilvie**

# The Hungriest Caterpillar

by

## ISABEL THOMAS

If hope were an animal, would it be a unicorn cantering through sun-lit clouds or a hippo that burps rainbows? Or could it be a creature that most people barely notice – a small, plain caterpillar, crawling on six stubby legs?

Our unlikely hero is the caterpillar of the wax moth, an insect with a very bad reputation. Wax moths like to lay their eggs in honeybee hives. When the creamy-white caterpillars hatch they tunnel deep into the honeycomb, chomping their way through beeswax, pollen and honey, and generally causing chaos. Scientists who study wax moths are usually looking for ways to stop them in their tracks. But one day, someone spotted that these caterpillars have a superpower.

Federica Bertocchini was cleaning out her beehives when she found a few wax moth caterpillars. Knowing they are bees' number one enemy, she popped them into a plastic bag while she finished the job. But she returned to find the bag full of holes. The caterpillars had eaten their way through the plastic and were making a slow getaway. Some people would have found them a tougher prison and forgotten all about it, but Federica is a scientist and she was curious.

She knew that plastic bags are made from polyethylene, a type of plastic so incredibly tough that blazing sunshine, biting wind, churning water and ravenous microbes take at least a hundred years to break it down. This indestructibility is why most of the plastic humans have thrown away is still piled in landfills, clogging up rivers and floating in oceans. How on earth had three small caterpillars destroyed a patch of plastic in just a few hours? Working with a team of colleagues, Federica began to investigate. They discovered something astonishing. The caterpillars weren't just chewing plastic bags into tiny pieces and pooping them out – they were actually digesting the plastic and using it as food.

The next step was to find out how. The world has herbivores, carnivores and omnivores, but no one had ever met a 'plastivore' before. Three years after Federica's discovery, another team of scientists found the second piece of the puzzle. Wax moth caterpillars have friendly microbes living in their stomachs. They usually help the caterpillars to digest beeswax – nature's version of plastic – but if their hungry host decides to eat human-made plastic, they're happy to switch. Together, caterpillars and microbes are an unbeatable team.

It would take sixty wax moth caterpillars a week to munch their way through a piece of plastic as big as your palm. They won't be able to solve the world's plastic problem on their own. But they give us hope that we can find solutions. If we can understand the wax moth caterpillar's plastic-pulverising powers, we might be able to copy them and find a way to break plastic up into particles that can be returned safely to nature.

The hungriest caterpillar is one story in a vast library that we're only just beginning to read. There is more hope hidden in nature's books and pages, waiting to be found. You can join the search. Next time you see something unexpected, pause, look closely, and let your curiosity show you which way to go.

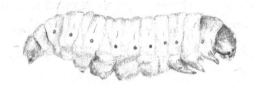

# Consider the Dung Beetle

by

## M. G. LEONARD

with illustration by

## CARIM NAHABOO

Is there any creature as mighty, as crucial, as funny and as downright adorable as the dung beetle?

You may think poo is disgusting, but in the natural world the nutrient-rich droppings of herbivores are more precious than gold.

The stoic scavengers of scat need exceptional strength, because even a small ball of fresh dung can weigh fifty times what the dung beetle does. The taurus scarab (*Onthophagus taurus*), a small oval beetle, black or rust in colour, with horns rising from its head like a bull's, is the world's strongest animal relative to its size and is able to pull 1,141 times its own weight – the equivalent to you dragging six full double-decker buses!

Most dung beetles can fly, and must, quickly, to get manure whilst it's hot. When an elephant unlooses a butt-load on the ground, four thousand industrious dung beetles will arrive to harvest the goodies within fifteen minutes – ten thousand within the hour. Collecting the dung into a ball, each beetle rolls the manure to a safe location, digs an underground chamber in which to hide it and then it eats it. And just think of how much dung is created every day! Why, one cow can do over nine tonnes of cowpats in a year! This is why dung beetles are a friend to farmers. They work tirelessly clearing muck that might otherwise attract bloodsucking animal pests.

Very few insects outside the community of a hive look after their babies, let alone form a family. But dung beetles are caring parents, building an underground nest and stuffing it with pellets of poop for their children to eat. There are some species (*Copris* and *Onthophagus*) in which both parents share the childcare duties – an excellent example for humans – and some (*Cephalodesmius*) mate for life.

To hunt the European minotaur (*Typhaeus typhoeus*), find sheep or rabbit droppings in sandy grass or heathland and search for tunnel entrances about one centimetre in diameter. Wave at hikers who will stare at you, thinking you are sniffing sheep stools, and smile, knowing you are hunting a mythical beast. The Minotaur beetle is the size of a rabbit dropping, with a glossy black exoskeleton, ridged elytra and a triad of horns on its thorax, which it uses to defend its tunnels. It hails from the *Geotrupidae* family, meaning 'earth borer', and its labyrinthine tunnels can reach over a metre in depth. The adults overwinter in pairs in their burrow, emerging in autumn to eat their fill of faeces before laying their eggs in their nest and provisioning it with poop for their young larvae.

The most famous beetle in the world is the sacred scarab, *Scarabaeus sacer*. Ancient Egyptians watched this fat superstar, with its burnished armour of black or bronze, rolling balls of camel dung across the sand and thought it an earthly mirror of Khepri – the god of the rising sun – whose daily task was to roll the sun across the sky.

Dung beetles have to be great navigators because rolling a giant ball in a straight line, pushing it from behind whilst standing upside down with your face to the ground, is not easy. They steer using the position of the sun or the moon, and on moonless nights they can navigate using the Milky Way.

Charles Darwin once wrote that to appreciate the magnificence of the beetle we should imagine it to be 'magnified to the size of a horse or even a dog …' How mighty would the dung beetle appear to us then?

# NATURE

Joy by Laura Hughes

# A-Viking in the Springtime

by
## JONNY DUDDLE

Oh, how I love the Springtime!
Night turns into daytime,
Makes me want to sing time,
Sun upon my cheeks time,
Skipping through the trees time,
Sailing over seas time,
A-Viking we will go time!
A-ringy-ding-a-ding time,
Oh, how I *LOVE* the Springtime!

# The Green Road

by

## KATHERINE WOODFINE

There's a path I walk, every day. A secret path slipping down along the side of a house, looking like it goes nowhere in particular.

It's an old path. Once, monks walked here, going down to the bay and back again, carrying the fish they caught and the salt they gathered from their salt pans. They called it the green road.

Once, peddlers walked here, carrying flax to market. Farmers walked here, on their way to the fields. It was trampled by animals' feet: the hooves of oxen going to plough or horses pulling their loads of night soil from the middens. Soldiers walked here: buried in the farmers' fields are old musket shots and cannonballs, as well as stone axe heads and Roman coins.

Once, smugglers walked here – or so they say – slipping up from the bay in the dark of night with their cargo of brandy and lace, carried secretly upriver from the sea. Some people still call it Smugglers' Lane. There are lots of old names here: Pony Wood and Piggy Hill and Teewit Field, named for the cries of the lapwings.

There are so many birds here. Goldfinches and blackbirds and wrens in the hedgerows. Coots and curlews and herons on the flooded fields; woodpeckers in the trees. In autumn, geese flying south for the winter or starlings massing. In spring, if you are early enough and stay quiet, you might glimpse a hare or a pair of young deer in the woods.

I've walked this path in every weather, and every season. In boots and in sandals. Counting magpies. Picking blackberries for jam, or elderflowers for lemonade. Watching the spring come in a haze of green buds on the trees; catkins, blackthorn blossom, then primroses and bluebells in the woods. The long lane turning white and lacy with meadowsweet and May blossom. Swallows and swifts in the sky, and the grass growing taller and taller, until the cow parsley waves high above your head.

In winter, the trees are bare and the hard ground glitters with frost. It is hard to believe in bluebells, or swallows swooping. But even on the darkest days, there are little birds flittering in the hedgerows. And so I trudge on, knowing as I do so that there will soon be buds on the trees, and catkins. Circling back on myself, following in the slow foot-steps of the monks, along the green road, down towards the water and back again once more.

Flower Power by Fiona Woodcock

# Waterfall

by
## JO COTTERILL

moss-furred
hobbit-stones
quilted-green

chuckle-cool
water-run
knobble-dark

laugh-smile
rock-splash
happy-child

# Butterfly Field

by
## JO COTTERILL

I have never seen
so many peacocks
in one place
eyes flashing
over, under between
petals of purple
leaves of lime
small suns on stems
and the peacocks
out-ornamenting them all
as if to say
we are so many
and so beautiful
that the rest of you
needn't bother

The Helping Hand by **Melissa Castrillón**

# THINGS THAT GROW

To plant a
**garden**
is to
believe in
**tomorrow.**
*–Audrey Hepburn*

To Plant a Garden by **Alex T. Smith**

# Sunflower

by
## GERALDINE McCAUGHREAN

Hal planted the seeds between the house and the shed without much enthusiasm. Everyone had been given three to plant and tend during the summer holiday: there would be a prize for the sunflower that grew tallest.

Hal knew he wouldn't win; Bogsy's would. He had told Hal as much. In fact, Bogsy had threatened everyone: *'I'd better win.'* The prize – a trowel – was not important: Bogsy just liked winning. He was a bully. At the very sight of him, Hal's shoulders would fold forwards, his knees bend; he was like those gorillas in the jungle – the submissive ones who grin and stoop while the big ones bite, screech and hurl baby gorillas from the treetops.

Hal planted the seeds, patted the soil flat.

Just one grew: a little sprig at first, then needing a cane to support it. It grew a flower. Hal said encouraging things, and it *almost* seemed to listen. But it never suggested what Hal could do next term to stave off Bogsy's pushes, punches or sneering insults. Sometimes, some lout passed by the back fence, kicked it, ran a stick along it. Bogsy.

Every day, Hal stood to attention in front of his sunflower: 'Keep growing, Sunny! Stretch up tall – like this, look. Grow till your head hits the sky!'

Weirdly, as Sunny grew more splendid, Hal grew less so. He kept tripping over things – all the time. His back ached, his knees crackled. Reaching for things, he knocked them over. Bogsy was right: he *was* a muppet, a bozo, a loser. But if Sunny could beat Bogsy's sunflower, *that* would be a kind of triumphant revenge.

Just before term began, Sunny lifted up her face – and stood taller than Hal.

First day of term. New blazer, new trousers, new shoes. Same old Hal inside. He dug up Sunny and potted her. 'Do you think she'll win, Dad?'

'Hope for the best,' said his father doubtfully.

Hal had to carry her to school: she did not fit in the car. He tripped – of course he did, useless muppet that he was. The pot spilt its soil. He walked on; flowerpot in one hand, sunflower in the other. As he knelt in the school garden, wedging Sunny back into her pot, Bogsy came up behind him. 'Where'd you nick that from, loser?'

Hal stood up, palms sweating, heart thumping. Bogsy looked him over, head to foot, and took a step back. Oddly, he seemed to have shrunk.

'Where's yours?' asked Hal.

'Couldn't be bothered.' Bogsy curled his lip – and took another step backwards.

Wobbler came past, wheeling his bike. 'Swipe me, Hal! You've *shot* up!'

The morning sun cast three boy-shaped shadows at their feet, long and dark ... Hal's was longest.

'Grow till your head hits the sky,' whispered Sunny. (Or did Hal imagine that?)

Sunny didn't win: another sunflower stole the prize by a centimetre.

But no boy stood taller than Hal.

# The One-Hundred-Year-Old Gardener

by

## P.J. LYNCH

The one-hundred-year-old gardener taps the bottom of the plastic pot with her trowel and slides the root ball of the plant into her cupped hand.

She has grown this and nine other young strawberry plants from seed on the shelf inside her kitchen window.

Kneeling on an old leather coat, she opens another hole in the soil in the sunniest spot of her garden. She carefully places the plant in the soil.

With her big thumbs she packs the ground firmly around the stem and splashes water around the young plants.

Two straight and even rows of five.

In two months she will pick the fat, shiny strawberries and she will carry them in a bowl back to her kitchen.

There will be enough to make two pots of jam.

But the next summer's harvest will be the best.

'When I will be one hundred and one!'

# That Peeling Feeling

by

## JACK NOEL

My grandad told me about an artist called Joseph Beuys. Joseph Beuys said: 'Every activity – even peeling a potato – can be a work of art.' This was in the 1960s, before the internet and oven chips, so they had a lot more time for things like peeling potatoes. But even so, I think I know what he means. I like peeling things too.

I like peeling:

- candle wax from the kitchen table
- PVA glue from my fingers
- potatoes when I'm helping Mum

And satsumas. I LOVE peeling satsumas.

Most days there is a point in the middle of the afternoon when Mum is off checking on my grandparents and my brother is off in the other direction, shouting over the garden fence, and I am alone. I like to go to the kitchen table and sit there, in between things. I'm not starving, but I am peckish. I'm not tired, but I am quiet. I'm not bored, but I'm bored enough to eat fruit on purpose.

Sunlight pushes through the open window, making the dust dance. I take a satsuma from the fruit bowl and hold it up. Birds sing. I look at the bumps and bulges, the pits and craters. An orange planet.

I start by biting. Sink my teeth into the skin, just to get it going. I get a sneak peek of the taste to come, like when you watch a trailer before you go to a movie. That first opening is a secret door to another world, like that cupboard that goes to Narnia. I work a fingertip into the opening. To keep the peel in one piece you have to kind of wiggle your hand as you pull. Micro-moves: up, down, back, forth. It's as neat and as natural as a turtle moving its flippers. A turtle on *Blue Planet* gliding through the shallows. The camera below, the sun shimmering above like a radioactive satsuma.

Sometimes I do this while I'm FaceTiming friends or watching the news or whatever, and I don't even think about it. But sometimes, when there's nothing else, I watch my own hands at work and see the orange skin fly free and it is kind of cool to notice. The fruit shedding its skin like Mum shrugging off her big blue coat after a long shift. The peel twists and turns over and over like a *Blue Planet* turtle showing its pale underbelly.

I pluck satsuma segments like petals, one by one. Before I eat them I watch them, one by one. Exposed, the sunlight makes their insides glow. They are full of light and zest and pulp and pips.

I eat them, one by one. It's just a satsuma. It's just a satsuma and I'm just a kid. Just a kid eating a satsuma in the middle of everything.

"Remember Peanut,
wherever a flower blooms,
so does hope..."

# Wherever a Flower Blooms by Rob Biddulph

# MORE AND
# MORE ANIMALS

New Classmates by Emily Gravett

# Shark Puncher

by
## JESSICA TOWNSEND

There was a girl in the ocean, waiting for a wave to surf. She'd been paddling for ages, when a very large shark leaped up and bared its very sharp teeth.

'My mum's a shark puncher!' the girl shouted, squeezing her eyes shut and waiting to be chomped.

Improbably, the shark paused. 'Your mum's a what?'

The girl blinked and felt a little strange, because a very large shark was talking to her.

'Shark puncher,' she repeated, trembling. 'She punches sharks. Professionally. She'll punch you to death if you hurt me.'

'Oh.' The shark bobbed in the water. 'That's mean.'

'Not as mean as trying to eat someone!'

He swam around her once, twice. She watched the fin and waited for teeth, pulling her legs in close.

The shark emerged again. 'Look. I was hungry. But you're right. If I don't want people to punch me, I shouldn't try to eat them.'

She thought he might leave then but he stayed, swimming in circles.

'What's your name?' she asked.

He glanced sideways. 'Sorry?'

'What should I call you?'

The shark's face didn't change, or not in any way she could decipher. 'Dunno what you're saying.'

She rolled her eyes. 'I mean—'

'Oh, like – OK, I get what you mean. I do have a – a thing, what'd you call it?'

'Name.'

'Right. I have one, but I don't think you could pronounce it.'

'Try me.'

The shark gave a strangled, guttural, gurgling roar.

The girl tried to copy him. She sounded like an upset donkey.

'Nah, it's more like –' The shark made the noise again. 'It sort of comes from the back of your – like this.'

He made the noise again.

The girl tried again. She sounded like an indignant walrus.

'Maybe I should leave it.'

'Yeah.'

He looked as disappointed as it was possible for a shark to look. 'It's probably just, like … a shark thing. You might not have the right mouth or whatever.'

They were silent awhile, listening to the distant cry of seagulls, each worrying the other had grown bored.

'You could give me a different name,' he suggested. 'I don't mind.'

'Really?' She sat up eagerly. 'How about … Leonard?'

'Leonard the shark?' He didn't sound impressed.

'Don't you like it? It was my uncle's name. I can choose something different.'

'No – no, it's fine. Your uncle's name. That's nice.'

'Yeah.' She dangled one leg in the water. 'I never met him, but my dad says he was a good bloke.'

'What's a good bloke?'

'Um. Just, like … a decent person. Someone you like.'

The shark seemed pleased. 'Do you like me?'

The girl smiled, showing her teeth. She thought he might understand the language of teeth. 'You did feel bad about trying to eat me.'

'I wasn't really – I wasn't going to eat you. Probably.' He paused. 'No, I was, I should be honest. I was fully going to eat you.'

'But you didn't.'

'No.'

'My mum's not really a shark puncher,' she admitted. 'No such job.'

Leonard expelled water from his nostrils. 'That's a relief.'

'Sorry I said that.'

'No, completely understandable.'

And Leonard swam for a bit, and the girl paddled, until a wave washed her ashore and they parted as friends, sort of, or at least neither eaten nor punched.

# Hare Time

by
## PIERS TORDAY

One animal that enjoys both solitude and spring is the brown hare. They can be seen, in late March and early April, sprinting after one another over the fields before standing upright on their long hind legs to take swipes at each other with their paws, as if they were humans having a boxing match.

This phenomenon gave rise to the phrase 'Mad as a March hare', which you may recognise from *Alice in Wonderland*. The mad hare is in fact a love-obsessed buck (male) who bounds after his beloved doe (female) and gets punched on the nose for his trouble. But these bouts are not as mad as they look. The does tend to be larger than the bucks and so by testing their suitors for strength and speed, they work out who will be a strong and healthy mate for them to start a family with.

About six weeks after they have mated, tiny leverets (baby hares) appear. Doe hares are unusual mammals in that they can become pregnant whilst *already* pregnant, a rare process known as superfetation. Once she has had her litter – typically around two leverets at a time – a doe will groom and feed her young for a few weeks, sometimes carrying a leveret around in her mouth like a cat with a kitten, before leaving them to fend for themselves.

After that, hares tend to be solitary creatures. Unlike rabbits, who live in a warren of burrows together, hares have no home. They dig shallow ditches in the ground to sleep in, called forms, in which they spend much of the day before emerging to consume vast quantities of food at dusk.

Legend has it that a hare crossing your path is unlucky, but today you should count yourself extremely fortunate if you see one. Brown hares were brought to Britain during the Iron Age and although originally revered as godlike – the modern Easter Bunny derives from the hare-headed Anglo-Saxon goddess Eostre and her pet white hare – they have also long been hunted for food.

So they are not only wary of humans, but practised at fleeing from them. They can run twice as quickly as the fastest human on earth, thanks to their huge, powerful engine of a heart and long, muscular hind legs. Speed is not a hare's only defence: they also confuse their predators by 'jinking' – sudden, breakneck zigzagging turns.

Perhaps it was this combination of speed and craftiness which gave rise to the folk tales told all over these islands in which witches transform into 'witch-hares' at night, accused of stealing milk from cows and nibbling saplings in orchards, among other crimes.

Who can say, but there is certainly something magical about these elusive creatures who have been spotted at night, all arranged in a circle and cast in silhouette by the milky light of a full April 'hare-moon', lost in silent parliament with one another for reasons that are, as yet, beyond our comprehension.

# A Golden Visitation

by

## ED VERE

Walking up hills does me good. Complaining leg muscles warming, reminding me of a different kind of alive. Long views from the top. Working out how this land lies. Sky. Air.

On a walk, if I remember, there's time too to sit – quiet. In a field, by a river, on the side of a hill. Somewhere no one is. When I've sat awhile, and been quiet awhile, that's when I hear and see. Really hear and see. The songs of birds, weaving around each other. Breaths of wind brushing long grass into silk. A trickle of water rounding a stone. When you are truly still, that's when nature shapes around you.

That's when you sense the slightest movement, over there in the undergrowth. When you hear the faintest, trembling rustle. When, in golden evening sun, you see emerge a mystical creature who rarely lets himself be seen. Over this low drystone wall creeps a shy beast, twitching, long-legged, magical, casting a spell over all. Someone wild and free who plays in the sun. Yards from me. He twitches, my breath is held, our curiosity mutual. Both wondering, *Who is this beast?* Then, this hare, all limbs extended, he flies – swift, powerful. A golden visitation, gone.

I think the same happens with us if we allow ourselves, for a while, to be quiet – to allow another a chance to approach, as their true self.

# Hope Is an Ancient Reptile

by

## SOPHIE DAHL

My younger brother Luke wanted a tortoise. He'd been promised one for aeons. Finally, on his seventh birthday, worn down, our mother bought him one from a local pet shop in Oxford.

When they arrived home, bearing a small, lumbering, prehistoric-looking creature with piercing, beady eyes, Mum asked Luke what he'd like to call the new arrival.

'TORTY,' Luke said. 'Obviously.'

'Oh,' Mum sighed, with a look of grave disappointment. 'Nothing a bit more sparky?'

'No. He's called Torty,' Luke said shortly, sweeping out into the garden, his pet clacking behind him like a rusty bumper car.

And so it was that the most interesting tortoise, with the world's least interesting name, arrived in our lives.

Torty was always a daredevil; an international man of mystery. In 1997, he ended up on a bonfire in the cardboard box he'd been hibernating in, after a clear-out of the garden shed. Our nanny, Maureen, saved him from the licking flames and when we opened his box, holding our breath, we found Torty, snug in a nest of hay, snoring. A couple of years later, he ran away and lived with the boy who lived five houses down from us for months. Luke had to give him a lot of Pokémon cards and a chocolate orange to get Torty back.

Once, a bird of prey tried to carry Torty off as he ate dandelions, clearly thinking he'd make a good dinner. Torty was a wriggly, scratchy captive and the greedy bird dropped him quite swiftly. After a few minutes of stunned silence, Torty began to munch again as though he was entirely used to large birds of prey scooping him up and dropping him from great heights.

For some reason, Torty ended up living with me about eight years ago. He lives inside in a big wooden house called a tortoise table, but on sunny days he loves to race around the garden and menace our cats and dog. If they're sleeping he sneaks up on them and nudges them with his head, hissing. This makes them leap up in horror. He also likes to creep up on humans and climb their shoes, and often does this to me when I'm writing. It always makes me scream.

Torty likes strawberry tops and cucumber, and I give him a bath, every day, in a funny old washing-up tub. He has a special vitamin powder in the water called REPTO BOOST and after he has soaked, I polish his shell with a little oil. He then walks around in circles, searching for the cats, a swaggering, oily gladiator.

He has run away seven times. The last time he ran away, he was found near the train station by a man named Trevor who was walking his dog late at night. Trevor's dog was sniffing away at a stone: a stone that turned out to be Torty. Trevor took him home and Torty had a sleepover with his pet rabbit. In the morning, a neighbour realised that this runaway was our tortoise, and rang us. We raced round to Trevor's house to collect Torty, who looked a bit sheepish with old strands of grass hanging out of his mouth.

When we got home, he crawled into his house and slept for two days straight. We call him the Reptilian Rambler. He is 79 years old.

# The Hope-o-potamus

by
## GREG JAMES AND CHRIS SMITH

In a drought, in the dust, in a dry river bed
A sad hippopotamus hung his grey head.
He'd had nothing to drink since the start of this week.
If he didn't find water things could get quite bleak.

The hippo was sad and the hippo was hot.
But did he sit down and give in? Of course not!
He remembered the words of a wise old giraffe,
That he'd heard long ago, when he'd been a young calf:

'There'll be times in your life when your road will be tough.
You'll be tempted to say that you've had quite enough.
There'll be people that try and convince you to stop,
And you'll feel that you're just about ready to drop.

'But those are the times when you've got to keep moving,
And with every small step you will see things improving.
Just point any way that seems hopeful to you,
You move one foot forwards, then foot number two.

'Then follow this up with your other two feet,
Then return to foot one, and repeat and repeat.
Remember these words,' said the wise old giraffe,
To our hero, the hippo, when he was a calf.

So the hippopotamus nodded his head.
'I'll keep plodding and see where I get to,' he said.
And he looked all around at the arid terrain,
And thought, *Will I ever find water again?*

Ahead, a high mountain rose up in the distance.
It looked rocky and steep, but with hippo-persistence,
He decided he'd walk till he had overcome it,
In case there were better things over the summit.

First he came to a desert, which wasn't too handy.
It was hard to walk through, rather slippy and sandy.
A camel was sitting on top of a dune,
And it told the hippo, 'You absolute loon!

'Turn around! Go back! Or you'll look like a chump.
There's no water this way, except this in my hump.'
But the hippopotamus shook his head.
'Just a bit further,' he boldly said.

One step at a time he continued his journey,
Till he came to a jungle – dark, dank, green and ferny.
The jungle was thick and the creepers were creepy,
And a large sloth hung down from a branch looking sleepy.

'This forest … it goes on for miles,' he said, yawning.
'Why don't you just hang here with me till the morning?'
The hippo – though tempted – again shook his head.
'Just a bit further,' he bravely said.

He plunged on through the jungle, and after a while
He arrived at the mountain – the ultimate trial.
Poor hippo was tired, almost giving up hope.
But – one step at a time – he pushed on up the slope.

The mountain was rocky and strewn with huge boulders;
The stones hurt his feet and the sun scorched his shoulders.
A lion sat there on a rocky outcropping,
And the lion called out, 'You're much better off stopping.'

But the hippopotamus shook his head.
'Just a bit further,' he proudly said.
His heart was so heavy, his feet were so sore,
But he climbed and he climbed – one step, then one step more.

And, just when he was feeling ready to drop,
He finally realised that he'd reached the top.
And a splendid sight met his eyes when he looked down:
A wide muddy waterhole, gleaming and brown.

He could see lots of sploshing – someone was there bathing.
A hippo! A friend! And they seemed to be waving.
And the hippopotamus nodded his head.
'I'm glad that I chose to keep going,' he said.

Then a voice from behind him called out, 'We were wrong!'
The lion, sloth and camel had followed along.
And the animals cried, 'You're more brave than the lot of us.
Hip hip hooray for the hope-o-potamus!'

Everything Crossed by Steven Lenton

# TRUE STORIES

# Silver

by

## HILARY McKAY

Long ago, before you were born, before the internet was invented, I lived in an old, shabby cottage. Three hundred winters blowing and snowing had left it battered, but still it was a good home.

Not just for me. Bats lived under the roof. Frogs visited the bathroom. There were mice in the walls, spiders everywhere. Often, the ghost who walked the village street hammered on the door. The door knocker was a lion's head holding an iron ring. *Bang! Bang!* it pounded on moonless nights.

Jackdaws nested in the chimney pots. They lived in the ash trees nearby; joyful, chattering birds. Although they never built in the chimney above the living-room fire, I often worried that a youngster might tumble down.

One day it happened.

On the roof, the parent birds called frantically. In the room below fell showers of soot. Trapped in the darkness, the fledgling cried; a desperate sound.

One day, two days, three.

The silences between the cries grew longer.

I shone a torch to try and guide him down. I made jackdaw noises. In despair, I opened the door to the village ghost but nobody came in.

On the third day he fell at last, a bird blotted out by soot. He was quite still, but when I began to bathe him he suddenly gasped and flickered into life. Two shining silver eyes gazed straight into mine.

There was a box ready for him and I put him there, with a saucer of soaked bread. An hour later, the saucer was empty and all around the edge, where he had reached in and out, were small sooty triangles. A neatly written message saying, *thanks*.

As he grew stronger he took over the kitchen, bathed in a pie dish on the doormat, ate cheese, minced beef, raw eggs and oats, used chair-back perches to learn to fly, roosted by my typewriter on the table.

But one day he saw me outside the window and hurled himself at the glass to try and reach me.

It happened again.

Jackdaws live in families. They take care of each other, calling greetings and warnings. They play together. Jackdaws need jackdaws, not people.

So we went outside. It was evening, the sky was pink and green. Clumsily, as if outdoor air were heavy, he flew to the garden wall. He looked very small. I didn't know what to do, but he did.

He shook his clean new feathers and called his fledgling call, and a miracle happened.

A jackdaw swooped down. Then another. The parent birds, come back. They spoke together. Then, one on each side, they guided him home to the roost in the trees.

All summer I saw him. His chimney-battered feathers made him easy to spot. He was never alone.

Now the cottage is rebuilt. Nobody has seen the ghost for years. But still in the ash trees the jackdaws gather, joyful, chattering. Just as they did before the internet was invented, before you were born, a long time ago.

# Moses and the Watering Can

by

## WILLIAM SUTCLIFFE

This is a very short (and completely true) story about a brave mouse who I met last summer.

For about fifteen years we have owned a cat called Moses, who was given that name because his fur makes him look as if he has a long white beard. The name suits him better than ever now because he is old and wise, and accepts no nonsense from the two skittish kittens who have become his housemates.

Last summer, one lunchtime we found Moses (who is normally a calm and placid cat) in an angry and agitated state. What was he angry with?

A watering can.

Just to be clear, Moses is usually on very good terms with all our garden equipment. We've never seen him get angry with a watering can (or a hose, or a spade, or a trowel), so I went to investigate. I examined the watering can closely, looking right down into its musty depths, and as far as I could tell it looked completely empty and not even slightly annoying.

I asked Moses what was up but he just looked at me as if I was an idiot, which is how he often looks at me.

We carried on with our lunch, wondering if our cat had gone mad. Through the window we saw Moses continue Operation Fight the Empty Watering Can. He pushed it around, scratched it, stuck his paw into it as far as he could and never let his attention waver for a second as he hovered beside it with the lethal focus of a hungry predator.

When we'd finished lunch, we brought Moses into the house, closed the door and went out to look again at the watering can. This time I noticed that the watering can had a detachable nozzle and when I pulled it off, what do you think I found?

You've probably guessed. Yes, right there, inside one of the only spaces in the whole garden big enough for a mouse, but too small for a cat's paw, was an extremely frightened mouse.

We coaxed the mouse out on to the lawn, which took a while, and the mouse looked up at me and the rest of my family. At first it didn't seem to know what to do, as if it couldn't believe it had been saved. After a while, my daughter picked him (or her – it's hard to tell) up and carried her (or him) to a flowerbed. We watched as the mouse slowly recovered itself and scurried away to safety.

Was this an unusually clever mouse, or just lucky? How did it think of that hiding place?

I often think of that mouse, especially now, because she (or he) reminds me that bravery often isn't about noisy heroics, but about patience and quiet resourcefulness. It must have felt like such a long and terrifying wait crouching in the head of a watering can, utterly cornered. But even though it must have doubted that escape was ever possible, that mouse did get away and found its way back home.

# The Zoom of Doom

by

## FRANCESCA SIMON

Where do you get your ideas? The truth is, you never know when a good idea is going to whack you in the face. Often, when you are least expecting it. What follows is the true story of how I got the idea for the 100th Horrid Henry story, *Horrid Henry and the Zoom of Doom*.

Some people look for trouble. Others have trouble thrust upon them. I shared my battlefield with the war correspondent, Christina Lamb, but not in Afghanistan. No, we met our disaster at … Wild Wadi Waterpark in Dubai.

Christina and I met years ago at the Dubai Emirates Airline Festival of Literature and decided, in a moment of madness, that we would visit the famous waterslide park. I hate heights and I'm terrified of roller coasters, so go figure. We fussed and flapped – where do we put our clothes? How do we handle money if we're just wearing bathing costumes? – until the festival organiser sorting our transport snapped, 'Christina, you're a war correspondent. I'm sure you can manage Wild Wadi.'

So there we were, at the park. We did the baby rides, and quite enjoyed them. Egging each other on, we decided to try one I will call the Zoom of Doom. We hopped in a rubber raft, which skidded about up and down walls as we plummeted to the bottom. It was terrifying, but we survived and basked in the admiration for our daring back at the festival. 'The Zoom of Doom? Wow, never dared go on that one,' was the unanimous chorus.

Cut to three years later. We're back in Dubai, this time with Nujeen Mustafa (the disabled teenage Syrian refugee Christina wrote a book about), and we bring her to the Wild Wadi Waterpark, along with her brother and sister, to help us manage the distinctly wheelchair-unfriendly terrain. Christina worries about drowning her after she has made it all the way from Syria to Germany in a wheelchair, but Nujeen loves it.

'Let's go back on the Zoom of Doom,' I say.

Christina and I get in the queue. The crowd are lining up for two different rides, and when we reach the top we head to the Zoom of Doom on the right. One of the attendants eyes us up for size and places us with two others.

'I don't remember them balancing the raft for weight last time, do you?' I ask.

'Maybe the regulations have changed,' says Christina.

We take our seats. I'm surprised to see seat belts. We buckle up.

The raft inches closer to the edge.

'Christina, I don't remember seat belts, do you?'

'No.'

We look at one another.

The rubber raft teeters at the top of the precipice. Just long enough for me to realise that we've made a catastrophic mistake. The slide we'd been on before was NOT the Zoom of Doom. We were trapped at the top of the scariest, most terrifying water slide at the park.

Then the raft swept over the edge. As we plunged through darkness in a straight vertical drop, I shut my eyes. All I could think as we shuddered and juddered around hairpin turns was, *One day this will end.*

I don't know how long that ride lasted. A month? A year? Perhaps in some alternate universe, we're riding it still.

*Horrid Henry and the Zoom of Doom*, dedicated to Christina, was published in the book *Horrid Henry Up Up and Away.*

# How I Fainted in Front of the Queen

by

## ROSS MONTGOMERY

I have a fainting problem.

I've had it for years – I even fainted head first down some stairs once. There's nothing weirder than standing at the top of a staircase and waking up face first at the bottom, with no idea how you got there except the fact your face hurts.

It's happened so many times now that I can see the warning signs. I'll get spots in front of my eyes, start feeling wobbly and I'll know I have to do something quick or else I'll pass out. Usually I just need to sit down, have some water, maybe take a jumper off if I'm feeling too hot … simple! A few minutes later I'm feeling right as rain.

Of course, back when I was seven years old, I didn't know about any of that.

I was a choirboy back then. Every Sunday, I'd go and sing in a chapel near where I lived. The chapel actually belonged to the Queen Mother (Disclaimer: she was the Queen's mother). Every now and then, you could peek at the front of the chapel and see the Queen Mother sitting in a special area reserved for the royal family. Once or twice you'd even see the Queen sitting there, which was always exciting!

Until the worst happened.

The choir was in the middle of a song. I was standing up, singing at the top of my lungs, wearing a full chorister's outfit – ruff, cassock, surplice … it can get really hot.

Suddenly I began to feel … weird. Nowadays, I'd know right away that they were the warning signs that I was about to faint – but back then, I'd never even fainted before! So when I started seeing spots in front of my eyes and feeling wobbly, I just thought, *Ooooh, that's interesting. I'd better keep standing up and singing.* And so that's what I did. I started to feel weirder and weirder and weirder, and then …

Nothing.

That's the weirdest bit about fainting – everything goes black, and for some reason you just go along with it. You forget that just a few seconds ago you were standing up, and go, 'Oooooh, that's interesting. Total all-consuming blackness. I guess this is my life now.' And then you suddenly remember – 'Hang on a second! Wasn't I standing up in a chapel a few seconds ago?' and then BAM! You wake up again.

'Ross? Ross, are you OK?'

That's what happened to me. I woke up on the floor of the chapel – I was lying on top of another choirboy. When I'd fainted, I'd taken out the boy standing next to me with my head. The choir had stopped singing – obviously – and the vicar was trying to wake me up. He helped me to my feet – you always feel awful after you faint, and really wobbly – and led me out of the chapel. Everyone stared at me as I went.

*This couldn't be any more embarrassing*, I thought.

Then I turned around – and saw the Queen, the Queen Mother, Prince Philip, Prince Charles, Princess Diana, Prince William and Prince Harry, all leaning out of the royal box to stare at me. That week, the entire Royal Family had decided to come to the chapel – and I'd just fainted in front of all of them.

Once you've done that, fainting down the stairs isn't so bad.

# The Gift of Time

by
## SITA BRAHMACHARI

with illustration by
## JANE RAY

Homage to Dr A.K. Brahmachari (1931–2008) and Iris

Our dad was a dad with a big smile, a huge heart and an easy laugh. He was also a doctor who travelled on a ship from India in 1959 responding to the call from 'The Motherland' to help create the newly founded National Health Service.

I have a photo (you might have something like it in your family archive) of not-yet our dad in a long coat, Marlon Brando style, so young and handsome with a full head of hair, at the moment of arrival, pigeons landing on his hands, standing with fellow doctors who had made that long journey together.

In the background is a mother holding a child paddling in a fountain. A mother and a child my dad might later treat in a hospital; or in his GP surgery working side by side with my mum, Freda,

a nurse. Or they might one day meet in a post office – yes, a post office … and if you're willing to pass the time of day with me, you'll see why!

When I look at that early photo of Dad, I have a thousand memories I could share of acts of kindness to patients that I witnessed every day as a child, but this one makes me think of now …

One day, when I was nine years old, I tagged along with Dad to the local town. He had letters to send to India at the post office. That 'Anyone want to come along with me on a little trip?' became a whole morning. He met an old lady in the queue. Frail but determined, she held a letter in her hand. 'On its way to Canada, Doctor!' she explained. 'For my newborn great-great-granddaughter's birthday.'

That woman's name was Iris.

My dad took her arm and enquired about her health. Leaving the post office, we walked her to her door and were invited in. 'We won't be long,' my dad assured a sighing me.

The tea, Iris insisted on preparing herself in china teacups painted with violets. She would not let Dad help her pour the boiling water into the chipped brown teapot she covered with a rainbow-knitted cosy. 'We can get a few cups out of this, Doctor!' she said, patting it.

Time slowed. A ladybird crawled into the daffodil trumpet on the table. There were pictures of her family on her mantelpiece.

The teapot finally emptied.

Driving home in our metallic green Beetle, Dad explained to me, 'I have known Iris all my working life and I don't think she has long to live.'

Two weeks later, I accompanied Dad on a home visit to Iris's door. When he returned to the car, tears flowed down his cheeks, as they did mine, as they do now at the memory of his words and gift – 'It was Iris's time.'

# MAGIC

# Sick Leave

by
## CLÉMENTINE BEAUVAIS

When my uncle was ill I crossed the park every day to visit him, and it made me notice things I hadn't before: some trees creak in the wind; a lady walked her parakeet daily; squirrels' fingers look like those of babies in prams. Babies in prams grow fast. My uncle's illness lasted two seasons.

Something else I noticed: statues have hair. I didn't know that before. Stone hair, like them, and very elegant – it blooms in curls or waves, never scruffy. There are many statues in the park, and all got hairier. Near the entrance stands a lady with raised hands, half-wrapped in just the slightest marble veil that drops in teasing folds. That lady, last September, had an elegant top bun; by April her hair had slithered down to her bum. She also had underarm hair, a compact nest of it.

I told my uncle, 'The statues in the park are growing hair.'

'Are they now?' He smiled, and coughed, and ate a slice of cheesecake.

I told him about the veiled lady.

'And the two angels near the fountain, you know? They had short curls before. Now they're long and wild. They look like rock stars.'

'Sounds cool,' my uncle twinkled.

An old lady fed the birds, often near one of the most dramatically changed statues: a man with a goat's lower body. That satyr was *already* very hairy: ripples of beard, head hair, chest hair and sheep-like frizzly legs. But by May, he'd practically turned into one of those Highland sheep with more fur than limbs.

'Have you noticed a change in the statues, recently?' I asked the bird-feeding lady.

'Sure,' she laughed. 'What's happened to the barber, d'you know?'

'The barber?'

'He normally comes every week. Poor statues! It's not as if they could brush their hair away from their faces, or tie it up. Some are stuck with fringes that reach down to their chins. '

So it was for the Three Graces near the ice cream van, who couldn't see a thing any more. And there was a colonel on horseback, someone very important, whose helmet had tilted to the side down a river of perfect locks.

My uncle started getting better in June. One day he called: he was completely cured, and today he would be walking across the park to visit us with homemade cherry pie.

He arrived with the cherry pie and a heavy box of tools that chinked and clanged when he settled it on the floor. My mother chided him:

'Be reasonable,' she said. 'You can't just begin work again so soon after such a long illness.'

'But my clients needed me,' my uncle pleaded. 'They needed me very badly.'

The next time I crossed the park, the statues sported neat new cuts. The barber had been, with his chisels and files. The lady with the veil had kept her underarm hair. Perhaps she'd grown to like it, and it did look very good on her.

# The Domovoi

by
## ZANA FRAILLON

*Listen.* This story has rules. Follow them …

**Rule 1:** Make yourself a burrow. Make one in your bed, or under a table, or between two chairs. Make one in the wardrobe, or in an old cardboard box. *Burrow well.*

**Rule 2:** Litter your burrow with things to *lure*. A photo or a book. Or that rock that you picked up that time and kept for some reason that you weren't altogether sure of … put the rock in the burrow.

**Rule 3:** Get paper and pens and pencils.

**Rule 4:** Believe.

Are you ready? Then go, into the burrow.

*Once upon a time …*

In every house, in every apartment, or tent or caravan or car, wherever a person calls home, there lives a house spirit. House spirits feed off words. Off night whispers and snippets of talk thrown from mouth to ear. They feast on arguments and gorge themselves on gossip and chin-wagging, nattering, messy, laughing chat. They swoon with the pleasure of riddles set, and poems performed, and tales told. And they

170

wait in hiding, waiting for someone to listen to the stories *they* have to tell.

Have you noticed your house spirit? Perhaps you thought the shadow shifting thicker under the window was a trick of the light. Or that the flitting image glimpsed on the very edge of seeing was just your imagination. Maybe you thought the padding footsteps or the soft knock on the window was merely the wind …

It wasn't. I *know*. I have met my Domovoi, my house spirit who lurks under floorboards and huddles in the stove's warmth. I have set my eyes upon his furred body, smelt his dusty scent, felt his weight heavy on my shoulder. I have heard his tales and imaginings breathed in my ear …

Remember rule number 4.

Here is something else I know. While you sit, cosy in your burrow, your house spirit is edging closer. Can you hear it? The soft scuttle of claws? Did you catch that snuffling, or the faint drag of a tail across the floor?

Your house spirit is with you now, in your burrow. Watching. Waiting for the words to tip from your tongue and delight. Can you feel the movement of air across your back? The tingle on your neck? Can you feel its whiskers on your leg; feel the touch of a warm, furry hand on your shoulder? Can you hear its whisper? See its snippets of stories bloom to life in your mind?

Perhaps you will do as I do and write down the tales your house spirit shares, or draw them into being. Perhaps you will imagine them, or dream them, or perhaps you will forget them altogether. Forget that the house spirit even exists. Until one day, when you see the place where the shadows gather, or where the light shimmers, just on the edge of your seeing ...

Now close your eyes. Your house spirit is waiting. It has so many wonders to whisper. *Listen ...*

# HOME ALONE?

Home Alone by Daniel Egnéus

# I Can Read Your Mind

by

## DANNY WALLACE

Hey, did you know that even though this is a book, and I can't see you, I can read your mind?

Did you?

No, you didn't.

Do you know how I knew that?

Because I can READ YOUR MIND!

I am a skilled mind reader, and this is the first mind-reading book. I am such a skilled mind reader, in fact, that I know EXACTLY WHAT YOU'RE THINKING RIGHT THIS VERY SECOND.

Do YOU know what you're thinking right this very second?

Well, obviously you do. If you didn't, it'd be weird. If you didn't, you would have roughly the intelligence of a courgette. And not one of the smarter ones.

But listen, Courgette Face, do you want ME to tell YOU what YOU'RE thinking when I tell you I am actually a very skilled mind reader?

You're thinking, *NO YOU'RE NOT!*

Am I right? Am I?

Of COURSE I'm right, because I am a VERY SKILLED MIND READER!

Now, let's make things interesting. Think about the very worst thing you ever did.

Go on. Think about that time you tripped up a nun or ate your cat's food or called a badger a very rude name indeed.

Think of it … NOW!

…

Oh my GOSH! I can't believe you did that.

Oh my GOSH! You are a terrible human being.

Oh my GOSH! Why would you think of that when you KNEW I would know?!

Does anyone else know you did that? Do your PARENTS?

Well, whatever you do, DON'T TELL THEM YOU DID THAT or they'll SELL YOU ON eBAY or swap you for somebody better behaved, like a BURGLAR!

In fact, let's pretend that never happened.

Try and think of NOTHING AT ALL. I want you to COMPLETELY blank your mind.

Wow, that was quick.

Not a lot going on up there, eh?

Well, now I want you to breathe. Deeply.

Breathe in through the nose, and out through the mouth.

Just relax.

And now close your eyes.

…

...

Hello?

...

HELLO? Why aren't you reading? **HELLO?**

Oh, I know what's happened.

Hey, OPEN YOUR EYES!

OPEN YOUR EYES AGAIN AND KEEP READING!

HELLO?!? OPEN! YOUR! EYES!

...

Well, that's great. You can't read that, so you've just kept your eyes shut. I mean, what am I supposed to do now? Just wait for you to come back?

Hang on. I know.

I'll read your mind again.

...

WHAT DO YOU MEAN, YOU THINK I'VE GOT ALL THE INTELLIGENCE OF A COURGETTE?!

I'm off.

So, just read the next piece in this book, and I'll TRY not to tell anyone you once tripped a nun and love eating cat food!

# The Ballad of Felicity Crow

by
## LISA THOMPSON

Felicity Crow had a remarkable skill.

She was an expert at not being noticed.

You might think that this is an unwelcome attribute or something to be embarrassed about. A person with a larger ego than Felicity's might say: 'How insulting! Can you imagine being so insignificant that you're not even seen?'

But for Felicity Crow, not being noticed was a compliment. It was something that took skill and time to master. And not being noticed was her job.

Felicity wasn't a pickpocket.

She wasn't a burglar.

And she wasn't a spy.

Felicity Crow was, in fact, a magician's assistant. Not only that, she was the best magician's assistant that anyone had ever not noticed before.

She worked alongside the great magician, Bertram the Remarkable; a man with a short temper and even shorter legs. He would strut around the stage, commanding all of the audience's attention as he promised the most magical of tricks, the most spellbinding of illusions. Every eye would be focused on him; transfixed by his dark, curly moustache, his big, booming voice and the solid-gold watch swinging hypnotically from left to right.

There was simply no attention left for Felicity.

But Felicity didn't mind. This was the part of the job that she loved.

Nobody noticed when she slipped a playing card into the pocket of a man in the audience.

'How did *that* get there?' said the man.

No one noticed when she released the cabinet's false door to make Bertram disappear in a flash.

'He's gone!' gasped a lady in the front row.

And nobody noticed when she passed Bertram a key that fitted the padlock shackled to his wrists.

'How did he escape?' whispered the audience to each other.

The magic worked because of Felicity Crow. She was unnoticeable. Even to Bertram the Remarkable.

He didn't notice her on stage when he spread his arms wide to receive the audience's applause.

He didn't notice her after the show when he placed her measly wages on top of the box of props.

He didn't notice her quietly practising her own card tricks in the corner, with a skill way beyond his own.

And he didn't notice her when she stepped out into the darkest hour of the night, clutching a deck of cards in one hand.

As she hurried down the city streets, a solid-gold watch bumped against her leg through her dress pocket. Unsurprisingly, Bertram the Remarkable hadn't noticed that it had disappeared.

She smiled to herself as she planned how she would dazzle an audience, all of her own. Her show would be magnificent and full of wonder and like nothing anyone had ever seen before.

Felicity Crow was ready to be noticed.

# Stronger Than Magic

by
## CERRIE BURNELL

In every time and in every land, there has always been something stronger than magic. Something that holds the same power as love and the rising brightness of joy.

It's like the feeling you get after a long bleak winter, when you see the first spring butterfly dance between flowers. Or when you go to sleep the night before your birthday with the promise of presents. Or you catch the scent of the sea and hear its crashing waves moments before you see it.

It's something born of moonlight and sunrise that has the same properties as a rainbow. And the littlest drop of it can help steady fear or make something that's impossibly sad seem ever so slightly lighter. It's an energy and a wish and a dream that can make you feel braver.

Its name, quite simply, is hope.

Think of all those familiar stories we know and how hope inspired them. The girl trapped in the tower without freedom or family. How frightened she must have been; how isolated. Yet still she stood at her window and sang. The hope of a better dawn filled her with joy. So she sang and she sang until her song filled the forest and reached the ears of a traveller passing by.

Or picture the boy, setting out alone, cutting down a forest of brutal thorns that none have ever found their way through before. It is hope that makes him keep going, believing that he will find the sleeping kingdom beyond the thorns.

Imagine the mermaid giving up her tail, finding the courage to venture into the unknown, into a world she's never seen. The wonder of new possibilities making everything seem magical, the hope in her heart giving her grit and tenacity so she refuses to ever give up.

Or remember the three children who found a shadowless boy and spiteful fairy and were told to think a happy thought, so they too might fly. Without those gorgeous memories, or hopeful wishes, they would not have risen into the air, nor turned right at the second star and flown straight on till morning.

Hope doesn't have to be vast or grand. It's not a spell. It's an enchantment we already have within us. On a sad or overwhelming day, when everything feels very dark, if you can find just a little drop of hope, a memory of something wonderful or a dazzling ambition, that tiny drop – no matter how small – will become your guiding star (or your second star if you one day learn to fly).

When the world seems dark or frightening, look for a single star. Make that star a hopeful thought. When you're ready search for another, until your sky is glittered with starlight – full of positive wishes. Then the dark won't seem as ceaseless and our dreams of a new future will be infinite and bright.

# Spells for Home

by

## STEPHANIE BURGIS

Wind battered relentlessly at the house on the hill. Outside the sleeping children's bedroom, the family cat batted and pounced through the night to protect them from every invisible danger.

In the heart of the house, the sorceress's study lights still shone from the computer on the desk. Shadows deepened under the sorceress's eyes as she worked, casting spells to her customers through the darkness.

But other eyes watched her from the corner of the room – eyes close to the ground and hidden in the shadows.

*Waiting.*

At last it happened. The sorceress tilted her head – stretched – then stood, lifting her empty teacup.

'One more hour,' she whispered to herself. 'Just one more cup.'

She left the room …

And the sprite, who had snuck into the house days ago, leaped for the desk, agile and long-armed as a monkey.

Not every child in the world has a mother to protect them. Some have to fight for their own safety.

This young sprite had studied the sorceress's household ever since she had wriggled inside, soaked and terrified, during another terrible storm. She'd meant to leave the next morning, but some impulse had held her, day after day, in this little house, despite its dangers. She could not hide forever from those thundering children's feet and the cat who stalked the house like a queen – but Bright-Eyes was clever. Careful.

A quick learner – and now she had a plan.

She tapped in the passcode she'd spied over the sorceress's shoulder.

The question on the website blinked out at her: *Name your heart's desire and the price you'll pay.*

'Anything,' whispered the sprite. 'I'd pay anything.' Her long toes typed the answer as her fingers tugged at her hair, sending gold dust flying.

A voice spoke behind her and sent her tumbling in surprise.

'Home?' Holding a steaming cup of tea, the sorceress quirked her eyebrows at the fallen sprite. 'Is *that* what you've been hunting for?'

Sprites were good at pulling shadows over themselves to stay hidden, but only unforgiving light spread at the sorceress's feet.

The sprite shivered as she pulled herself up on to all fours. 'You … knew I was here?'

'No one enters this house without my knowledge. But how did you lose your own home, little one?'

'Our nest,' whispered Bright-Eyes. 'Builders. Cruel machines …'

The sorceress knelt. 'I can't give you back what's been destroyed.'

Bright-Eyes hugged her arms around herself. 'You *said* name my price. I'll pay anything!'

'You want the impossible.'

'Not any more.'

Bright-Eyes had watched and listened to everything in this house that stood strong against storms.

'I want *this* to be home,' she said. 'I'll stand guard in your shadows. I'll fight for you, if you let me stay!'

The sorceress looked down at her for a long moment, as wind battered against the outer walls. Then she sighed. 'That won't work for me.'

Bright-Eyes nearly crumpled. 'But ...'

'You see,' said the sorceress, 'in this house, children like you *sleep* at night and let me take care of their safety.'

Warmth filled Bright-Eyes for the first time in months. 'I can do that, too,' she whispered.

Outside, rain joined the wind lashing viciously through the air. Inside the house, though, from that night onwards, Bright-Eyes slept in her own nest, and no storm could touch her.

# The Hummingbird's Smile

by

## SOPHIE ANDERSON

There is a legend that glowing hummingbirds live in the deepest darkness of the maze. If you find one, the sorrows in your life will fly away
and you'll smile so joyfully that all who see you will fill with happiness.

Every year, children slip into the maze to search for the birds.
Some return downcast, having found only empty corridors swathed
in gloomy shadows. Others return with tales of grotesque monsters,
defeated by acts of great bravery. None, however, return with the
hummingbird's smile.

Until she was eleven, Nadia had no desire to go into the maze. But
when her little brother lost his favourite toy, he missed it so intensely
that nothing could comfort him. Nadia loved her brother and ached
to make him happy. So she set off to find the legendary hummingbirds.
She carried a ball of her mother's yarn, tied one end to a rock outside
the maze then stepped inside.

Darkness closed around Nadia. Cold squeezed her chest. But Nadia
pulled her shoulders back, clutched the yarn tight and strode onwards.

Whispers swished near her feet. Icy tendrils snaked down her neck.

Sour scents and low groans slid from ominous tunnels. The further Nadia crept, the more her heart thumped with fear.

Nadia didn't feel the yarn snap, nor did she feel it slip through her fingers. She only felt the sudden emptiness it left in her hand. Her tether home was gone. Lost, terrified, alone in the darkness, Nadia crawled on hands and knees, desperate to find the yarn. When her fingers closed around a strand she rose, elated. But the piece was just a torn fragment.

And yet … Nadia stood in the desolate dark and imagined how she might use it. Could she weave a compass to point the way home? Divine her way with the thread, like a dowser using a twig to find water? Or make a snare to trap one of the unseen creatures that pattered by, then ask for its help?

Plan after plan wound into Nadia's mind, all spun from one loop of yarn. None were perfect, but she kept dreaming, believing that if she did, she would think of a way to get home.

When hope stirred inside Nadia, she heard a noise from within her ear. A soft creak. A gentle crack. A rustle and a tickle. Out from Nadia's ear flew a tiny hummingbird, with shining green and blue feathers. A smile bloomed on Nadia's face, radiant with joy.

The hummingbird grew, larger than Nadia. Light and warmth thrummed from its buzzing wings. It nudged Nadia, until she climbed on to its silk-soft back. Then the bird zoomed from the maze, carrying Nadia, whooping with delight, into the brightness of the sky.

Far below, Nadia's brother saw the hummingbird, and his sister flying on its back smiling the hummingbird's smile. His eyes lit up, his sorrow flew away and he filled with happiness.

# FAIRYTALES, OF SORTS

# A Box of Pencils

by
## GILLIAN CROSS

Ella sat in the kitchen, beside the hearth. Her sisters were at the prince's ball, and she was hungry and bored. And hoping.

*FLASH!* Her fairy godmother appeared in a whirl of light.

'Don't worry, Ella!' she chanted. 'You *shall* go to the—'

'No!' Ella shouted. 'Not the ball!'

'What?' Her godmother stared. 'You don't want the dress and the glass slippers and … You know how the story goes.'

Ella nodded miserably. 'The prince falls in love, I drop the slipper and – I have to *marry* him!'

Her godmother frowned. 'You don't *want* to marry him?'

'Of course not!' Ella said. 'He never does anything except eat chocolate and shout at his servants. And he's *fifty-two years old*! If I marry him, I'll never go anywhere exciting. Never see anything new.'

'Hmm.' The godmother bit her lip thoughtfully. Then she gave a brisk nod. 'Right. Fetch some water and make a cup of tea.'

'You won't …' Ella looked nervously at the pumpkin in the corner and the lizard on the wall.

'Of course not!' her godmother said impatiently. 'Just get the water!'

Ella picked up a bucket and went out to the well.

When she came back, her godmother had disappeared. But she'd left two things on the kitchen table – a pad of drawing paper and a box of coloured pencils. There was a message on the first page of the drawing pad.

*Make yourself a cup of tea and start drawing.*

Ella filled the kettle and hung it over the fire. Then she took out a blue pencil. Very carefully, she began to draw the outline of a small, rocky island. Cliffs and bays. A harbour. A long, rocky point where birds might nest.

She took out a green pencil to mark forests on the map, and a yellow one to colour the sandy beach.

By the time the kettle boiled, the island had deep caves and secret tunnels, a cabin in the woods and a castle high in the mountains. Ella made a cup of tea and then – using all the colours in the box – she drew a coral reef in the sea.

What else? She sipped her tea, looking at the map. Suddenly, she knew what to add. Finishing the tea, she picked up a black pencil and drew something on the beach. Then she put the map on the floor.

'Thank you, fairy godmother!' she whispered.

Closing her eyes, she stepped on to the island.

Even before her eyes opened again, she knew she was really there. She felt the wind on her face and smelt the scent of the sea. And there on the beach was the black wetsuit she'd just drawn, with the mask beside it. She put them on and waded out into the water. Gulls swooped overhead as she dived. And when she reached the reef, fish came swimming to meet her, surrounding her with all the colours of the rainbow.

Dragon Towers by Sarah McIntyre

# Gurgle

by

## SIBÉAL POUNDER

Everyone knows the Tooth Fairy is called Gurgle.

She doesn't particularly like the name, but she can't imagine it being anything else now.

Everyone knows being a tooth fairy was not her first career choice.

She always hoped to be an astronaut, but they said she was too small.

She doesn't even really like teeth. They are a little dull for her. In an interview with *Dentists' Weekly* she said she would like them much more if they were rainbow-coloured.

She can always paint them.

She does enjoy finding fun ways of getting into children's houses. Once she rode in under the ear of a dog.

She doesn't want to talk about the time she had to enter via a toilet.

She pays a lot more money for good teeth because teeth with holes are more likely to collapse when exiting Earth's atmosphere.

And a tooth with a hole won't hold up against alien attacks.

She has a hole in her own tooth. It happens. Her toothbrush has cat ears on it and she's going to fashion the same style for her helmet.

She puts an advert in *Dentists' Weekly*, looking for someone to cover her tooth fairy duties while she's away.

'No previous experience with teeth required. Must like children.'

Two full-sized humans excitedly reply to the advert.

They are looking for a career change.

Gurgle thinks they are both a little big – they would never be able to sneak in via a toilet or under a dog's ear.

But she hires them anyway, because everyone deserves a chance.

On her final shift, she pays a handsome price for a perfect tooth. 'Knocked out on the swings,' the note says.

She paints it purple and adds it to her creation. It is now complete.

The two humans agree, the rocket made of teeth looks much better than a normal, boring rocket.

Gurgle beams as she thinks of all the children who helped create it (and the swings). She's proud of her rocket.

And so she should be – it travels faster than a normal, boring rocket. Gurgle hits outer space in five seconds and is soon well past the moon.

She decides she will write to NASA upon her return and give them some tips.

Many children spot the rocket, and some adults too. It looks like a streak of rainbow light shooting through the night sky.

Just think – your teeth might be in space right now.

# Jack and the Ram

by
## SALLY GARDNER

Jack lived with his mum in a small bungalow on a ribbon road just outside town.

Jack had wanted a lamb for his birthday. His aunt had sent him one from Cardiff.

The lamb was small and sweet. Jack bonded with the lamb; wherever Jack went, the lamb went too.

To the shops.

To football practice.

To school, where the lamb stayed outside the classroom making notes.

The lamb grew into a ram. He could read, write and count sheep.

Mum often heard Jack talk to the ram. But Mum was a grown-up, and grown-ups know that sheep can't talk.

One day, Mum bought some magic beans from a fortune teller in town; guaranteed to make any wish come true. But before Mum could plant them, the ram munched them all up!

That was the last straw. The ram would have to go, so Mum said.

That night, the ram, who could speak English and a tad of French, wished that he was a unicorn.

The next morning, the ram looked into the bathroom mirror and there it was in the middle of his forehead; a unicorn horn.

'Wow!' said Jack. 'That is ace!'

'I could really rock the flock with this,' said the ram.

His mum shouted as she went to work, 'Jack, take that ram to market.'

'But it has a unicorn horn,' said Jack.

Mum wasn't listening.

*Parents*, thought Jack, *can be tough.*

Before they set off, Jack took a picture of the ram and its unicorn horn and put it on Flockergram. He wrote that they would be at the market today. They packed sandwiches and set off.

Market day was always full of people and animals. Jack was wondering where best to show off his ram when a woman cried, 'There it is! I saw that ram on Flockergram!'

By now, people had begun to crowd around them.

'Is that a real horn? It's not stuck on?' said a little girl.

'It is stuck on,' said another man.

'It isn't a nice thing to do,' said a lady. 'Sticking a unicorn horn on a ram.'

That's when the ram said, 'Ma'am, this is my horn, grown all by myself.'

Everyone stopped.

'Did that ram speak?'

'Yes,' said Jack. 'He's been speaking for ages. No one believes a ram can talk, but they do believe it might have grown a unicorn horn.'

Mum said, when she saw Jack and the ram return home from the market, that she was pleased he hadn't sold it.

'We could have done with the money,' she said, 'but it's good to have a ram about the house.'

The next day, the ram looked out of the window to see a film crew.

'What are they doing here?' asked Mum.

'They're probably here to sign up a talking ram with a unicorn horn,' said Jack.

'Well,' said Mum, 'who would have imagined that?' They opened the door on to a brand-new best beginning.

# Little Red Wolf

by
## L.D. LAPINSKI

Many years after Mama hung up her cloak with the red hood, the wolfskin on the rocking chair we kept on the porch began to lose patches of fur. Cats were suspected. Then birds, perhaps picking the fur off to use in their nests. The wolfskin looked faded and sad, the still-attached head of the wolf staring mournfully out at us with its glass eyes. They said it had been poorly cured, that we should throw it away. But we didn't – we held on to it, even letting it inside the house.

I liked the wolfskin. When Mama wasn't looking, I used to balance the wolf's head on top of my own and creep about the house, a girl in wolf's clothing, scaring dolly-woodcutters and cotton-wool sheep. I lowered it down, so the glass eyes were level with my own. All the better to see them with!

In our house, the wolf was what you got warned about. Be good, they said, or it'll get you. But the wolf was my friend, my disguise, the soft cover on the splintery old rocking chair. Who's afraid of the big bad wolf? Not I.

And, when it fit me enough not to drag on the ground, I pulled Mama's red cloak on, the hood over my head. And I went into the forest, basket in hand, following the path that led to Grandma's house. Grandma's house was a ruin now, the old stone and wood long since abandoned when we all moved into the new houses in the new town, away from the forest and away from the wolves and away from the stories.

I stepped off the path in the forest, and felt the dry needles move beneath my shoes. My red cloak glowed like fire in the sunlight that dared move between the trees. My basket felt heavy in my hand. Mama's warnings whispered fiercely at me as I walked on, into the growing gloom.

There was a low growl. It started deep in the chest of a wolf, and threatened to come to a halt in my throat. But I stayed still, watching as the wolf-mother glared at me from her den. Behind her were four pups, all of them bright-eyed and beautiful.

The smallest of them had a coat of red fur.

I had heard the woodcutters and the huntsmen talking, you see. I had listened to them planning, threatening, plotting against the wolf-cub with the red coat. The runt of the litter, it would be easy to find in the woods, easy to catch as it struggled to run in its mother's wake. A little red wolf, following the path, waiting to be tricked. And what big teeth it would have, if they did nothing.

The wolf-mother met my eyes.

I pushed back the hood of my red cloak.

The wolf-mother stopped growling. I don't know if wolves have stories, but she knew who I was. I was a wolf in girl's clothing. The

198

wolf-mother regarded me with axe-sharp eyes. She listened to the shouts of the men chopping through the trees, and she understood why I had come.

The grey wolves ran into the forest, blending into the shadows and disappearing from view in the thickets of protective thorns.

And some minutes later, I walked out of the forest with a wonderful treat in my basket. A tiny baby wolf with a red fur coat, coming safely through the forest to be taken to its grandma's house.

# Blanket

by

## NICOLA SKINNER

I was eight. Dad was at the wheel, steering our car through the wintry moorland while dusk crept towards us. Gesturing at the cold wild dark outside, he said: 'If you were lost, here, and couldn't find me or Mum, what would you do?' (This was in the 1980s when no one had mobile phones apart from five Americans, none of whom I knew.)

Within seconds, I felt sure of my answer. 'I'd knock on the door of the nearest house.' My parents nodded approvingly. Encouraged, I went on: 'And ask to borrow a blanket.' Ignoring their surprised looks, I added: 'Which I'd wrap around me and then wander across the moor, till I found you.' There was much to admire in this plan, I thought, especially the borrowing of the blanket, which felt daringly sophisticated and also practical.

My older brother shot me a pitying look, then gave *his* reply. 'I'd knock on the door of the nearest house too,' he said. 'But *I'd* ask to borrow their phone.' This, admittedly, was something I hadn't considered. 'I'd phone the police, ask them to pick me up and bring me back to you.' It might have been dusk, but I could see his winning smirk clearly enough. He had won this hypothetical survival task, and I was all alone in the moors with only a fictional blanket to my name. His answer was obviously the best.

Now, though, I'm not so sure. Although my idea may not have protected me from hordes of wildebeests, if I had lived to see the dawn, I would have had the greater adventure.

Children are often taught that being 'lost' is a bad thing, an experience to cut short as soon as possible. And losing *things* is something to be avoided completely. Like hope. 'Don't lose hope,' is the rallying cry when times are tough. 'We must never lose hope.'

But I disagree. Losing hope is as normal as losing a sock. I lose hope regularly. Some days I wake up and it's right there; others it's nowhere to be found, not even in my back pocket where a lot of other things end up.

But if you lose hope, it doesn't mean that hope has lost you. I think hope *likes* to be lost, so it can bring back stories, dreams and adventures, plans for better days, promises of star-lit nights. Hope is full of wanderlust, and must occasionally roam far from us in order to fulfil its true purpose. So, if you can't find your hope it's probably just exploring, looking for treats, just like a bird, searching out the juiciest berries to bring home to you.

Yesterday, I saw my hope by a riverbank admiring a tyre swing that hung, quite still, over the water. She saw me and said: 'One day, children will come back to this tyre swing and they will play across the river all afternoon,' and she sounded so sure about this, I felt immediately better about things. And then I asked if she wanted to come back with me, as it was getting cold.

'No, I'm good,' she said, pointing to a fictional blanket that I faintly recognised, which was now draped across her shoulders. 'I've got this.'

# Anna Bailey

by

## SALLY NICHOLLS

When Anna Bailey's mother was killed by an incendiary bomb, nobody knew what to do with her.

'Don't you have relations?' said Mrs Brady. But Anna's father was at the bottom of the English Channel, and there was nobody else.

Mrs Brady was the lady they'd evacuated Anna to. She was thin and sharp and twisted like barbed wire, and Anna hated her.

'She'll have to go to the children's home,' Mrs Brady said. But the home had been shut up, and all the children evacuated. So Anna stayed in Mrs Brady's dark little cottage peeling the potatoes, scrubbing the steps and reading fairy stories by the light of the oil lamp.

Mrs Brady's cottage was on the lane to the manor house, which was a hospital for wounded sailors. One day, as Anna was picking raspberries, a sailor came past her gate. He was tall and slender, with a vivid scar across his cheek.

'Good day!' he said. 'May I have a handful of your raspberries, for I'm very hungry?'

'They're not my raspberries,' said Anna. 'But I don't mind.' She knew what it was like to be hungry.

'My thanks,' said the sailor. He noticed that her hair was lank and greasy, and fell into her eyes. She noticed that he spoke like a person in a fairytale.

The next time he passed, he gave her a silver handkerchief to tie up her hair.

'What fine gooseberries you're growing!' he said. 'Please may I try them?'

'Of course,' said Anna, and giggled. He noticed the bruises on her arm that looked like fingermarks. She noticed that his hair was green at the tip and curled like tree roots.

The next time, he bought her a little cake the colour of moonbeams.

'Please,' he said, 'may I try some strawberries? And why are you crying?'

'I'm only tired,' said Anna, but he noticed that her shoes were tight and worn through at the heels. She noticed that his eyes were silvery-grey and seemed to sparkle in the twilight.

That night, Mrs Brady found a pair of red shoes, wrapped in dock leaves, lying on the doorstep.

'A grown man and a little girl!' she raged to the hospital matron, while Anna wept. 'It's not right!'

They searched the hospital for a sailor with curly hair and grey eyes and a scar across his cheek, but found nobody.

'Little liar!' said Mrs Brady, and she locked Anna in the coal cellar.

That night, the roots of an oak tree grew into the cellar. The stones broke apart. A clear blue stream flowed through, growing deeper every moment until it became a river. Fish swam around Anna's toes and a sailor on a barge of cedar floated by.

'Come,' he said, and held out his hand. And Anna went.

When Mrs Brady unlocked the cellar door that morning, Anna was nowhere to be seen.

# ALIENS AND
# OUTER SPACE

Very little information is available about this planet.
It is the most distant known world in our solar system.

# Northampton, 1968

by

## Mark Haddon

# Hello

by
## POLLY HO-YEN

They arrived on a Tuesday morning, just after morning break. Mr Egon didn't notice at first, the light being blocked from the room as the shadow of their spaceship filled the sky.

We were sent home as soon as someone could collect us. Our class got smaller and smaller until I was the only one left. They hadn't been able to get in touch with my nana.

'I can walk myself,' I said. I usually did that anyway.

I could see the teachers wanted to go.

It felt like it was night outside, it was so dark. It was either too quiet because most people were staying inside or too noisy; the people I met were shouting loudly, like they were on full volume.

I was almost home when I felt it: a flash, a freezing, a thousand bubbles rising up inside my brain. Then a voice came from inside my head that was not my own:

*Hello.*

I didn't answer.

*I know you can hear me.*

Who is that?

*I'm what you would call one of the aliens.*

But, how—?

*It would take too long to explain … Just accept that
we are communicating.*

*We want to know more about this planet and its
dominant species, the human.*

I'm human …

*Good! I've been waiting for a human for some time now.
I keep getting squirrels.*

Squirrels! Did they say anything back?

*Yes. This communicator allows me to converse with
any sentient being on your planet.*

What did they say?

*The squirrels?*

Yes.


*I can't really say … There are confidentiality issues.*
*Tell me what you think about humans, Human.*


I'm Marnee.


*What's marnee?*


That's me, that's my name.
What's your name?


*We don't have names like you do. I am identified by a sort*
*of very short song that cannot be translated.*
*But for the purposes of this, I will adopt a human name.*
*You can call me Wendell.*


I like it. Hello, Wendell.


*Hello, Marnee.*
*Tell me this: what's important to you, as a human?*


That's a **big** question.
I don't know where to start.


*Just say the first thing that comes into your head.*


211

My nana.
She looks after me.

*What's she like?*

My nana?
She's the kindest person in the world.
And she always knows how to make me laugh.

*Interesting.*
*What else? What else is important to you?*

So many things. Big things – like the environment – but then
sometimes it feels important to eat chips.
Does that make me sound silly?

*Maybe a bit.*
*But this was helpful.*
*Thank you.*

Are you going now?

*Yes, I have to collect more data. Goodb—*

Wait!
Why are you here?
What are you going to do?

*I told you – we're here to learn about humans.*
*You've taught me a lot.*
*Goodbye, Marnee.*

Goodbye, Wendell.

They had left by the time I got home.

Nana had heard an alien too. They'd asked her the same thing.

Her answer had been me.

# First Contact

by

## LOUIE STOWELL

My mum is a politician, which means I have to go to lots of hyper-boring events with even more boring adults. On the plus side, she's an *intergalactic* politician, so at least the hyper-boring events are in space. Her current mission is to make first contact with a new species of alien. Excited is not a big enough word for it. I'm going to meet ALIENS!

Apparently, this particular planet has been through some tough times lately, so we're bringing a bunch of supplies – medicine, tech … I forget the rest. I'm still waking up, really.

We've been asleep for most of the voyage, but the pods opened this morning and we're landing later today. Mum says it's important to have a while to prepare mentally for a new planet. Also, the pods leave you smelling of weird disinfectant so I wanted time to take a shower. No one wants to meet a new alien species smelling like the med bay floor.

Freshly scrubbed, I went for a walk around the ship. I'm the only kid here but Mum let me bring my pet robot, Blinky. I called it that because it's got one sensor light that blinks on and off when it needs recharging.

'Oh! You are awake!' said Blinky, as it flew down the corridor towards me. 'I have missed you!'

I don't know if robots actually CAN miss you, or if it's just pro-grammed to say that, but I like it anyway.

I stretched out my limbs. It felt great. The pod sends little waves through your muscles to exercise them, and adjusts your position, but there's nothing like a real-life stretch.

'Let's go and see the planet,' I said.

On the viewing deck, the planet spread out below us. We were close!

I knew from my lessons that it was a blue planet, like ours, with vast oceans and a breathable atmosphere – well, mostly. We have to take pills to filter out some of the harmful chemicals, but we won't need masks.

My lessons had never brought home how beautiful the planet was. Blue water, high mountains, green plant life.

'Just think, Blinky, we'll be walking around down there soon,' I said.

'Technically, you will be bouncing. It's a very low-gravity world compared to ours,' said Blinky.

I was excited about that part – not just the bouncing, but the fact that I'd be super strong compared to the aliens! Not that I was planning to show off or anything. I was mostly excited to talk to some other kids again! I'd been learning their language, and even a few alien jokes!

'PREPARE FOR LANDING!' said the ship's computer. It was time. I went and found my mum and we got into our seats.

The seat belt bit into the green of my skin as gravity hauled us down into the atmosphere.

Below us was the beautiful new alien world. The aliens who live there call it Earth. I can't wait to meet them.

HEY YOU! YES YOU! Right now, while you munch on your BREAKFAST some MIND BLOWING stuff is happening... UP there, in SPACE!

MOONS and STARS CEREAL

Spaced Out by Kate Pankhurst

# HOPE FROM
# A DIFFERENT
# PERSPECTIVE

# Lost

by

## MICHELLE PAVER

The young wolf darted into the thicket. He was exhausted, terrified. His forepaw hurt. From many lopes away, the human had pointed the kill-stick: an ear-splitting crack, fierce pain savaging his paw.

How had he got to this terrible place, far from the mountain where he lived with his pack?

Chasing the buck had been *fun*. Leaping logs, turning nimbly on tireless paws … Then the buck had bounded across a strange, smooth trail, and the wolf had lost its scent. He'd tried heading back, but he couldn't; huge, shiny boulders were roaring past. They had great, glaring eyes and a nose-biting stink, and always more came screaming, faster than any wolf could run. Their trail was smeared with the carcasses of badgers, squirrels, crows.

That was when the faraway human had pointed its kill-stick – *Crack!* – and the wolf had fled to the thicket. He'd been in here too long, he had to get out.

He raced up a hill, dodging a herd of big, blotchy creatures who shied from him with panicky moos.

Another boulder screeched to a halt and a human jumped out, raising a kill-stick. *Crack-crack!* But the wolf was gone, zigzagging between bushes.

He spotted the mouth of a cave, sped inside. Horses in the gloom, snorting in alarm. Outside, the clumsy footsteps of the big male with the kill-stick.

No way out. The wolf was trapped.

He sensed eyes on him.

Not a pounce away crouched *another* human. The wolf smelt that she was half-grown, startled. She raised her forepaw. She was holding something: a kill-stick?

Hope fled. The wolf slumped down. It was over. He would never see his pack again.

Instead of a crack, a faint click. No bite.

The wolf raised his head. *Click-click-click*. Like a woodpecker.

The half-grown female lowered the kill-stick that wasn't a kill-stick. She bared small, blunt teeth in an uncertain grin. She'd been eating blackberries, they'd stained her muzzle and forepaws. The wolf remembered the same thing when he and his sisters were cubs.

The big male had nearly reached the cave. His bark was angry, searching.

Turning her head, the half-grown female yelped a reply then quietly moved to the cave wall – *and pushed it open.*

Was it a trap? She was nodding, pointing. The wolf shot past her into the light.

The barks of the big male faded. The wolf was back at the roaring trail, boulders racing past – but not as many. With the last of his strength he leaped … He landed on the other side.

The boulders' roars sank to a growl. The wolf waded into a river and drank, cooling his flanks, his throbbing paws.

His pack was calling to him. Raising his muzzle, he howled a wobbly reply.

As he started up the mountain, he saw in his head the half-grown female who liked blackberries, and had helped him escape.

Q: Can you guess what the half-grown female is doing with what she's holding in her hands?

A: Taking pictures with her phone.

# A New Sun-Up

by

## BEN BAILEY SMITH

Brody couldn't believe his luck.

Big Boss Gary was there, Big Boss Nadia was there ...

His whole team was there too: Team Member Max, Team Member Layla and Tiny-New-Guy Pedro. I mean, Tiny-New-Guy Pedro was there most days *anyway* – and to be totally honest, Brody had felt as though both Big Bosses and Team Members alike had been a *little* over-focused on the latest arrival.

Recently, it had seemed that whatever Pedro did, the rest of the team would react. He would scream and they would run about. He would cry and they would take him to the park. He would moan and they would get him dinner. *Ten times every sun-up*, it felt to Brody!

When Brody moaned or cried, the results were rarely the same as that.

Still, Tiny-New-Guy Pedro was both an official Team Member and a New Smell and Brody loved him, he supposed.

Was it the attention or the food Brody had been upset about? He couldn't remember. You see, Brody's memory was a little hazy now because *time* had changed.

Every five sun-ups there used to be two sun-ups when the team was all together and he would run with them, playing games and going to places that had food and drink and treats and cuddles and more running and new smells.

Now every sun-up was the same ... *or was it?*

The whole team was there. Every sun-up, doing different things in different combinations:

- Big Boss Gary, Team Member Layla and Brody digging holes in the garden. For ages. *Brilliant.*
- Big Boss Nadia, Team Member Max and Brody emptying out a massive cupboard with a smell he'd never smelt before. *Quality.*
- Big Boss Gary, Tiny-New-Guy Pedro and Brody walking round and round on wheels until Pedro went silent. *Can't argue with that.*

It reminded Brody of those other sun-ups from before this time: the ones where they went to live in a field for a while, in a tiny triangle house made of cloth; the ones where there were huge, brown eggs as big as your head that made him sick and Layla cry; even the cold ones with all the singing and the *outside* tree *inside* the house!

It was incredible really: *Food, cuddles, runs, walks, exploration, new smells, long chats, team games, movies with cats in them ... Every single sun-up!*

*What a time to be alive*, Brody thought.

He'd heard from friends that Tiny-New-Guys like Pedro often led both Bosses and Team Members to ignore Bigger-Not-New-Guys like him.

For now, though, Brody felt more important than ever. At any given time the food was plentiful, the cuddles were longer and there appeared to be no shortage of cat movies.

And for an old dog like Brody, *that* was a perfect sun-up.

# Hope is the thing with feathers
### EMILY DICKINSON

Hope is the
thing with feathers
That perches in the soul
And sings the tune without the words
And never stops at all

And sweetest
in the gale is heard
And sore must be the storm
That could abash the little bird
That kept so many warm

I've heard it in
the chillest land
And on the strangest sea
Yet, never, in extremity
It asked a crumb of me

Hope Is the Thing with Feathers by Chris Mould

# The Creature in the Cave

by
## JENNY McLACHLAN

When I was nine years old, I found something truly incredible.

My mother had taken me exploring, as she often did, and we stumbled upon on a beach. It was a small curving bay with pebbles and a patch of sand. While I poked around in rock pools and swam in the sea, my mother stretched out on the warm stones and soon fell asleep.

This meant I could wander further.

I was scrambling over some boulders when I discovered the cave. It was hidden behind a curtain of leaves; inside, the light was green and the air had a tang of salt and fish. I thought that the cave led nowhere but then, at the very back, I found a tunnel. I crept into the gloom and something crunched under my feet. Shells? I didn't know. I was a little frightened, but kept going because I was nine and this was exciting and ahead I could see a dot of light.

The dot grew bigger. It became a circle, an opening, I smelt the sea and heard the crash of waves. I had found another cave, but this was not the incredible thing I wanted to tell you about.

No. Something was sitting inside the cave.

I'm old now, and these are distant memories, but I will try to describe exactly what I saw that day.

The creature had a mouth and eyes, like me, but that is where the similarities ended. Its skin was so thin that I could see tiny veins filled with blue blood running down its neck. It was small, fragile and had claws so stubby they couldn't have opened a clam. It was colourful – its eyes were one colour, its hair another.

The creature swallowed. I could see its heart thudding under that thin skin. It was scared of me, and no wonder. Even then, I was big and strong. But then the creature did something incredible. Even though it was scared, it smiled and reached out its hand.

What happened next? Incredibly, we played. We drew patterns in the sand. We looked for stones. We dug a hole and watched it fill with water.

That happy hour ended when I heard my mother calling for me.

Back on the beach, I burst out of the tunnel and blinked into the sunshine. I rushed up to my mother, but didn't mention the creature. I didn't want her to say I was making it up, or worse, go looking for it herself.

Side by side, we ran along the beach, stretched out our wings and lifted up in the air. The wind rushed over me and the sun warmed my scales. As we soared higher, my heart soared too, because I was certain that the beautiful, brave creature in the cave was a human.

Humans belonged in stories told around the fire ... but I had met one!

I let out a roar of joy, and my flames lit up the sky.

# Hope Hunter

by

## JOSEPH COELHO

Hope Hunter had a secret. It only started being a secret when she realised, to her dismay, that no one else could see what she could see and that if they were to discover her ability, she would most likely be shipped away to some lab and tested. She knew the drill. Hope had seen all the movies.

Hope Hunter could see people's thoughts. They showed plainly on their faces, changing them completely. When a person had nice thoughts, their faces became radiant and started to physically change. Her teacher, Miss Bridges, was one of the kindest people Hope knew; some days her face would bloom like a flower with big blousy petals, other days it had the flittering wings of a butterfly. One time, when the class had been working for weeks on the Christmas play, Miss Bridges' face was a constellation of fireworks. Hope tended to be upbeat because, no matter what, she could always see the good in the people around her.

Occasionally, however, she did come across someone with horrible thoughts; it was rare and often fleeting. One time, Bradley and Pablo started fighting at lunchtime. Bradley's face had grown bat wings and Pablo had a tornado riding the crown of his head, but the teachers soon intervened and by next period Bradley's face had puppy fur and Pablo's looked carved from oak. There was, however, a girl in Hope's class whose face was always surrounded by thick spider legs.

Her name was Stacy and she was always alone. Hope avoided Stacy because she imagined that her thoughts must have been terrible to have spider legs around her face, dancing like witches' fingers. Hope was sure that Stacy was a nasty person.

One unfortunate day, Miss Bridges asked Hope to work with Stacy making a miniature book for a project. Hope wasn't scared of what she saw, she had seen enough strange things with her gift, but she didn't like it. Stacy barely spoke and when she did it took great effort, with the spider legs creaking slowly open to allow her thin voice to say 'Yeees' or 'Noooo' when Hope asked what colours she wanted the pages or what thread they should use for the binding. But bit by bit Hope found that the spider legs stayed open for longer and that more words would spin forth. Before long, they were chatting. Stacy opened up, revealing more about her home life, some of which was very sad, and Hope listened, noticing how lovely Stacy's eyes were under the spider legs. By the end of the session, Stacy had told Hope so many things, deep and secret, that Hope had found herself sharing her secret for the first time and it felt good. When Stacy asked Hope what she saw when she looked at her, Hope realised that Stacy's face had changed. That it wasn't thoughts that she saw, but feelings. 'Your face is incredible,' said Hope. 'It is crowned in the most fantastic shimmering silver threads.' And it was.

# The Sky-Bots

by

## VASHTI HARDY

In a place where shafts of golden light sliced ice-topped mountains, two sky-bots flew like slim feathered clouds, their shadows flitting across the liquid gleam of the lakes below.

'Where are we going?' asked Ardra, the smaller of the two.

'There's a creature on the mountain,' said Vreer.

'A creature?'

'Indeed. It's rather small, skinny and ...' Vreer shook her head and shivered.

Ardra glanced sideward. 'And?'

'Featherless.'

Ardra's wings juddered. 'But how does it keep its mechanisms from freezing?'

'It might have to be retired, unless we can help.'

They landed on the mountain opposite and observed for a moment. The creature huddled, shivering in the snow.

Ardra flinched. 'It's not of this world, is it?'

'I don't think so,' said Vreer curiously. She sniffed the air. 'But we shouldn't be afraid. Come on, let's get closer.'

As silent as breath they flew to land beside the creature, who hunched and drew back.

'What are you?' asked Vreer.

The creature stared, utterly perplexed, then stuttered, 'I'm ... I'm ... Martha Salisbury ... from London.'

The sky-bots looked between each other.

'London?' asked Vreer, instinctively weaving her tail behind Martha to keep her from shivering.

'It's a large city, with lots of tall buildings and buses and roads and ... stuff.' Martha shrugged.

Ardra wrinkled a nostril. 'It sounds very strange.'

'How did you get here?' Vreer drew her tail closer to Martha's back and turned up the warmth of her feathers.

Martha shook her head. 'I'm not entirely sure.'

Vreer nudged Ardra and pointed a silver claw at the sky. A strange rectangular shape, which Vreer thought to be the size of a small charging cell, punctured the sky horizontally above.

Martha followed their gaze and peered upwards.

Beside her, Ardra gently prodded Martha with the tip of her tail. 'Not completely featherless, Vreer. She appears to have been created with some flat feathers.'

Martha frowned. 'They're my pyjamas.'

A chill wind speckled with snowflakes washed through the mountains.

'It's very primitive weather protection,' said Vreer.

'I suppose I should climb back,' said Martha.

Ardra extended a paw in the air to help.

'Oh, thanks,' said Martha, looking up into the dark, rectangular space. She shuffled her feet for a moment. Hope and possibility shot like fireworks inside her chest.

Vreer darted a glance in the direction of the distant crystal forest. She whispered in Ardra's ear, then turned to Martha. 'Unless you'd like to take a ride first?'

They flew along silver streams, into valleys where magic murmured in the shadows, across diamond beaches, past trees heavy with the chitter of insectoids and through showers of luminous raindrops.

As night fell, Martha climbed back through the dark space in the air.

The sky-bots watched as she looked back. The shape fluttered in the mountain breeze as though formed of many delicate layers.

'Same time tomorrow?' asked Vreer.

With a grin, Martha nodded, waved, then took the opposite edges of the rectangle and gently closed it.

*Can you guess what the portal might be?*

# CRIME AND
# DETECTIVES

# The Wagatha Christie Conundrum

by

## SHARNA JACKSON

Five animals who would make distinguished detectives
– a study by Nik and Norva Alexander

**Introduction and background**

My sister Norva (13) and I (11) solve crimes and misdemeanours that occur on The Tri, the estate where we live. We have a strong success rate and have served justice to two murderers thus far.

The inception of this study dates from 31/10 (Halloween) when Norva dressed Ringo (our Jack Russell) as 'Wagatha Christie' – a canine costume that paid homage to the famous mystery writer.

Evidently inspired by her own creativity, on each of the following 164 days, Norva asked, 'Which animals would make sick sleuths?'

It is generous to state that 50% of her suggestions were unfeasible and the other 50% aggravating.

To quickly conclude the discussion, the ranked list below was formalised.

## Research methods

For the purpose of this study, the natural habitat of each animal was *not* taken into account, to ensure consistency across comparisons.

Please note: comments on the list are Norva's. Clearly Norva's.

## Results

### #5 Dolphin

Did you know that dolphins chat to each other without actually saying, like, dolphin *words*, but by making a wide range of sly sounds and moving around? A bit like me, to be honest. Seriously – how cool would that be in a sticky situation with a perp? Blink yourself out of a bind? Covert comms for the win!

### #4 Chameleon

Clever, colour-changing chameleons can cause chaos by blending into backgrounds and seriously spying on your behalf. Imagine – they could go *anywhere* and listen to *everything*. Also – they not only change colour to conceal, but also to show off – a hot look when you've caught your culprit. Stunt on those criminals.

### #3 Squirrel

Squirrels would crack cases like they crack nuts – easily. They totally have cute thief energy – so who better to catch one? These guys are straight-up sneaky. If they think someone is scoping out the location of their scran stash, they perform a 'fake funeral', then bury their food elsewhere. The misdirection! The drama!

### #2 Lyrebird

Our Australian bird buddies take mimicry to mind-blowing levels. They're out there in the outback, copy-pasting any sound they've ever heard – and pulling it off perfectly. I saw them on TV doing car alarms, camera shutters and crying babies. Imagine the situations they could get you in – and out – of.

### #1 Octopus

Eight arms (which grow back? Amazing!), three hearts, no bones: these flexible friends are multitasking masters – exactly what you need in a sleuthing sidekick. Imagine camouflaging yourself *while* squeezing through a lock *while* shooting ink as a distraction? Legendary. I stan.

**Honourable mentions**
* Pig – could save your bacon by being super smart – and not stinky
* Elephant – mammoth memories

**Intentional omission**
* Owls – overrated

## Conclusion

After intense research and deliberation, our study has determined that an octopus – if it had the ability and willingness to work – would make an excellent detective. Norva is inspired by this and claims she is actively seeking the services of one to replace me.

# The Comfort of Crime Fiction

by
## ROBIN STEVENS

When I'm sad, I read murder mysteries.

This might seem a bit strange, but I promise you it isn't. Murder mysteries are exciting, terrifying, shocking and twisty – but all of those scares and surprises only work because we always know absolutely that everything will be all right in the end. The murderer will always be caught. They will always be punished. Everyone else (apart from the murder victim, whose death always matters) will be safe, and the world will go back to being OK.

There is no problem in a murder mystery that can't be solved. Only one thing ever goes wrong at any one time, and ordinary people can take care of it. It's all gloriously simple compared to the real world, which, I've realised more and more throughout my life, refuses to follow the rules of a mystery story. Big, bad, unfixable things have a way of happening around me, and that can be difficult to get my head around. And that's why I write murder mysteries as well as read them.

When I write my Murder Most Unladylike Mysteries, I'm creating a world where good wins, where wickedness is punished and where even the smallest people can make a huge difference. It's the world I'd like to live in, a world I still believe is there underneath all the confusion, and it's a gift I'm giving to my readers. You're allowed to step away from messy, bewildering reality and live safely with my detectives, Daisy and Hazel, for a while. Dark and terrible things happen to them all the time, because a world without dark and terrible things really would be a fantasy. It's impossible to know you're happy if you don't remember what it's like to be sad. I need to let my characters look monsters in the eye – but I always know they can defeat them.

Detectives like mine are hopeful characters. They save people, they fix every problem they come up against – they are good and brave and (whether or not they always show it) kind. Watching them solve each case, I hope you know you are in safe hands. I hope they make you ready to step out of the world of my books back into the real one, better and braver and more kind – and more able to face whatever life has to throw at you.

# PLAYTIME

Where there is a Dream
there is Hope.

# Where There Is a Dream, There Is Hope
## by Petr Horáček

# Football Boots

by
## PETER BUNZL

The boots had plastic studs on,
that raised me off the ground.
On the tiles in the changing room
they made a clacking sound.

Out on the playing field
they grasped turf in their grip,
but when I crossed the tarmac,
they always made me slip.

I wore the boots for football,
every Monday week,
in rain and snow and sunshine,
in fog and hail and sleet,

I teetered as I ran along
through grass and clag and mud

and kept my eye out for the ball,
which landed with a *THUD!*

Eleven boys tore at me then,
churning up the field,
and the coach he screamed: 'JUST KICK IT, SON!
... YOU, BOY, MAKE THE STEAL!

'HEADS UP, YOU LAZY LEMONS!
MAKE A BLOOMIN' WALL!
PASS THE THING!
MARK YOUR MAN!
EYES ON THE FLIPPIN' BALL!!'

My boots would get all muddy
as we ran around and round,
and when the game was over
we had to scrape them down.

And when that task was finished,
we went inside to change,
and as I put my boots away,
we'd talk about the game.

'Some sterling play!' the coach would say.
'You lads have done me proud!
Get showered now ... And quiet, boys,
it's getting FAR TOO LOUD!'

Chalk Drawing by Rebecca Cobb

# The Greatest Gift

by

## MAZ EVANS

There's a buzz inside our cupboard
A tingle in the air
'They're coming,' whisper teddies
As the dollies brush their hair

Your jigsaws are in pieces
Your chemistry is set
Your water pistols cannot wait
To get somebody wet

It's the moment we were meant for
That long-awaited day
The greatest joy of all we toys:
When you want us to play!

We've waited in our boxes
Or lingered in a pot
We've sat in darkened corners
All the toys that you forgot

But now you're home together
The day has finally come!
'Let's play that game,' we hear from Dad
'Where is that toy?' says Mum

So make believe you're pirates
Or be a puppeteer
Or learn to knit that fluffy scarf
That Santa brought last year

We arts and crafts are standing by
To make the world look better
So why not help us spread the joy
And send us in a letter?

We board games are all ready
To host an epic fight
(Just make sure that your adults
All play fair and stay polite)

We're just so glad to see you!
We're always standing by
To help you fill your days with fun
And make the hours fly

We might be gifts from birthdays
Or gifts from Christmas time
But now we get the greatest gift
The gift that is your time

Lost in Music by David Roberts

# The Demon Goalkeeper

by
## ALEX WHEATLE

I missed a penalty last week
My teammates gave me some cussing heat
Told me I was too cocky with my fancy feet.

Our left back called me a clown
Felt like getting out of town
Couldn't buy a nice word
For a penny or a pound
Standing on a football pitch
Never felt so down.

Didn't attend school on Monday
Took a bedroom holiday
Pulled the covers over
Wanted to wake up at the end of May.

Mum sent me back to school in the morning
She had enough of my faking
Sitting in maths
Heard the penalty jokes
And the laughing.


Went to see the manager after school
Told him I wanted to give up football
He shook his head
And told me not to be a fool.


He said it's the big game at the weekend
Semi-final of the Cup
On you we depend
One disappointment
Is not the end.


And I want you
To keep taking the pens
So, keep your head up
And practise
Again and again.

Asked Dad to take me to the park
Didn't care that it was getting dark
Shot after shot
Dad saved them all
Apart from one penalty
That went over someone's wall.

Dad had enough
He called me to go home
We'll find your ball with a drone
I couldn't laugh
Or raise a smile
My confidence was shattered and blown.

Night after night
I practised on my own
Aimed to the left
And to the right
Felt a little better
In the twilight.

The day of the big game
Followed by a cloud of shame
Didn't think I could bear it
If I got the blame again.

Their goalkeeper was the best in town
No one better around
A demon between the sticks
It was like trying to score
Against walls of bricks.

Half-time whistle blew
They had a few chances
And we had a few
Their demon goalkeeper saved everything
That wasn't anything new.

Still level with a minute to go
I burst down the right
Their left back was too slow.

Sped into the box
Nutmegged the defender
Cunning as a fox
The right back knocks
The ref pointed to the spot.

Me against the demon goalkeeper
He filled the goal like a bus
He saved penalties without much fuss
His giant hands were another plus.

I ran up to the ball slow
Didn't want the demon to guess which way I'd go
Everyone stood on the edge of the D
Decided to keep the ball low.

The demon dived to his left
Wouldn't have mattered if he went to his right
My placement was deft
Straight down the middle
In the back of the net the ball came to rest.

Teammates jumped all over me
Including the left back who called me a clown
The manager took us all out to dinner
Said I was the best penalty taker around
Demon spot kicker of the town.

Apples and Swings by David Tazzyman

# AMAZING
# MACHINES

# Jeddi's Attic

by

## AISHA BUSHBY

Jeddi's attic can travel through time. Don't believe me? I'll prove it.

All I have to do is climb up the dusty old ladder, and try not to fall as it wobbles, and suddenly I've entered a whole new world. There are boxes filled with jewellery, and pieces of furniture, and clothes that haven't been worn in years.

Most people are afraid of attics because they think they're filled with spiders, or ghosts, or worse. But the truth is, attics are filled with magic. And only those brave enough to go searching will find it.

In case you're wondering, *jeddi* means 'grandfather' in Arabic. Which reminds me – have you ever heard of a grandfather clock? If you haven't, you can look it up online, or even in an encyclopedia.

Now that we've cleared that up, have you ever heard of a jeddi clock? You won't be able to find one online, or look it up in a book, because it's a secret. But Jeddi won't mind if I share it.

Up in the attic everything is covered in dust, too. I walk over to the jeddi clock, and on the face, instead of just the time, there's the day, month and year. All I have to do is set it to the day, month and year

I want to visit, then I climb back down the ladder and … I've travelled back in time!

Today I think I want to go back to the first weekend of spring, where I spent the day baking cookies, and dressing up, and playing with my pet cat.

You might think that's a boring day to pick. After all, I could pick *any* moment in the history of time. I could pick the summer holidays, or my birthday, or even back when the dinosaurs roamed. But sometimes, the very best days are the ones spent at home doing the silliest of things. And right now, that's exactly what I want to do.

You can try my jeddi clock, if you like, and we can travel back in time together. I'll even let *you* decide where we go next.

# The Washing Machine That Went to the Moon

by
## DAVID SOLOMONS

The washing machine gazed up through the laundry-room skylight.
A year had passed since the engineer's visit – tonight was the night.

'There's more technology in one of these,' he'd said, with a tap on its
  casing,
'Than in the rocket that went to the moon.' Which set its mind racing.

It would take one giant leap for domestic appliance.
Like the man said, it was only rocket science.

'You've got a bearing loose,' the vacuum cleaner wheezed,
And all the small cleaning appliances joined in and teased.

'You're going nowhere,' the steam mop hissed – there was almost a riot.
Then the old dryer slammed its door and the laundry room fell quiet.

'When I were fresh out the box,' it creaked, 'I made a voyage me-self,
Crossed oceans to get 'ere, braved waves as 'igh as that shelf.'

There were murmurs of doubt, but the dryer was old school,
Had a tattoo to prove it. On its casing was: Whirlpool.

Sure, the dryer was ancient and full of hot air,
But grateful, the washing machine began to prepare.

Baffling buttons and dials covered its outside,
Their function a mystery, even with the owner's guide.

Surely some combo would send it to space,
But even it couldn't figure out its own user interface.

Then came the breakthrough, the solution unorthodox,
The fuel for the mission, a mixed hoard of odd socks.

And at last launch day came, time for the show,
It ran through pre-flight checks, go or no go.

Initiate prewash sequence, detach primary cold-water hose,
Begin countdown, remove final load of clean clothes.

Ten, nine …

Soon it would set levelling foot on lunar ground,
A better place than this to spin around.

Eight, seven …

And proudly plant a flag in the traditional manner,
The 'Formerly White Shirt on a Field of Stray Red Knicker' banner.

Six, five …

The washing machine gazed up, its drum whirring louder,
The moon in the skylight, round and white as a scoop of laundry
    powder.

Four, three …

This was a chance none would say it had squandered,
Soon it would report: 'Houston, the Eagle has laundered.'

Two …

The door lock engaged, the drive motor spun
And the countdown reached …

One.

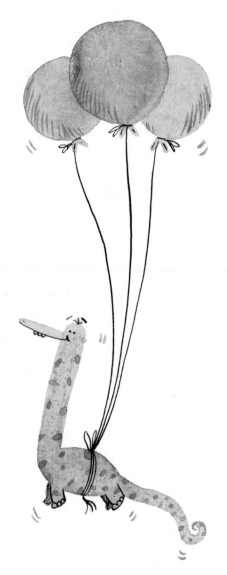

# We Can Fly by Rikin Parekh

# The Hope Machine

by

## SAM COPELAND

Let me tell you – it's not easy being an Evil Supergenius when you're ten years old. Firstly, nobody respects you or your evil plans. Secondly, my Evil Supergenius laugh sounds more like a giggle because I still have quite a high voice. Thirdly, all the adults have already copyrighted all the cool superhero and supervillain names. So – and do not laugh unless you wish to die – my alter ego is … The Deadly Pencil. Trust me, I tried every possible combination of names and they were all taken. And my superhero nemeses are Sensible Boy, Captain Coventry, and Llama Boy and Goat Girl. Also – the movies are wrong. There are *so many* superheroes. It's so tiresome – *everybody* wants to be a goodie. I'm completely outnumbered. They all get to hang out together and I'm completely by myself. But that's how I like it.

So, I have to come up with evil schemes and that's why I invented the Hope Machine. If you hadn't guessed, it's a machine which makes hopes come true. Dangerous technology if it fell into the wrong hands though. Can you imagine? It would be all 'world peace' this and 'love and happiness' that.

Yuck.

The first time I attached the Hope Machine's mind-reading helmet, I closed my eyes and hoped that something horrible happened to Goat Girl (she had just foiled one of my evil schemes), and it worked *perfectly*. I found out the next day that one of her goats had eaten her cape and pooed in her helmet.

The second thing I hoped for worked so well it backfired. I hoped I would finally get some respect and that I'd be treated like a proper Evil Supergenius. The following day I woke up to find my house completely surrounded by superheroes. And not just Llama Boy – all the big ones were there. They insisted I come out and apologise for being naughty and I had to promise to behave from then on. I had no choice but to agree.

So undignified.

The final time I used the Hope Machine was the night before my birthday. After the embarrassment of having to apologise, I decided to finish them once and for all; I hoped for DEATH TO ALL SUPER-HEROES! I went to sleep wearing the Hope Machine helmet just to make EXTRA sure my hope came true.

That was a very bad idea.

I awoke the next day to the doorbell ringing. I answered it to find all my nemeses on the doorstep.

They were *not* dead.

They were very much alive and carrying balloons and cards and presents. All for me.

There was a cake, and they sang 'Happy Birthday' and they gave me a huge party with games and dancing.

It was all perfectly *dreadful*. Clearly, the machine had gone horribly faulty while I was sleeping and for some reason thought I hoped for fun and happiness.

Now I'm stuck with having *friends*. And I even caught myself *smiling* this morning – and it wasn't even a supervillain evil grin.

Double-yuck.

Obviously, I have thrown the Hope Machine in the bin.

# DRAGONS, AND SEA-DRAGON MILK

# First Flight

## by
## KATIE AND KEVIN TSANG

The baby dragon watched from her cave as her mother and all the other dragons in her clan flew off into the sky. She sighed wistfully. She too wanted to fly.

But she wasn't ready to fly yet. Her mother said she wouldn't be ready until the next full moon. The baby dragon squinted up at the sky where the moon was already out. It was a half-moon. The baby dragon huffed. Surely that would be good enough.

She did a little hop. There. That was practically flying. She hopped again, and this time spread her wings. When she sat back on her haunches and spread her wings, they stretched high above her head. But she had only just grown strong enough to fully open them and she was still getting used to them. They didn't feel like they belonged to her, they felt borrowed. Like she needed to grow into them.

But wings were wings. She hopped again with a little more force. This time she stayed airborne for just a moment.

*Aha!* Now all she had to do was flap. Surely that was it.

She did a few tentative flaps. Her efforts sent dust flying up in the air all around her. She was surprised and pleased at her own strength. *I can do this*, she thought. She started to flap harder and promptly fell over, scuffing her snout on the cave floor.

*Hmph.* She looked around, glad the cave was empty and none of the other dragons had seen her.

Flying shouldn't be so hard. She was made to fly. She had even done it in her dreams.

The baby dragon went to the edge of the cave and peered out. She was high up. Very, very high up. A gust of wind blew past, tickling her ears.

Wind! That was what was missing. The wind would help her fly.

She took a deep breath. She could do this. She was a dragon. Everyone knew dragons flew.

She backed up a little bit and ran as fast as her small legs would go towards the edge and then, without thinking twice about it, she leaped into the air and spread her wings.

She was flying! She squeaked in excitement.

Wait. Perhaps she was falling … not flying.

She flapped faster and faster, straining her neck to keep it as high as it would go. She could do this! *Fly fly fly*, she whispered to herself.

And then a gust of wind from below lifted her up, filling her wings like a sail. And she soared across the sky.

Then she glanced down. Her mother was flying beneath her. The baby dragon suddenly realised it was the force of the air from her mother's giant wings that was keeping her aloft. Still. She was flying. And it was wonderful.

Her mother flew higher until the baby dragon gently landed on her back.

'You are very brave,' said her mother. 'But next time you want to fly, wait for me.'

# An extract from *Mold and the Poison Plot*

by
## LORRAINE GREGORY

Now we're finally standin in the cosy guard room Beetle just keeps peerin at me like I'm some sort of bug he aint never seen before.

'Why's he got such a big nose?' he asks finally, his voice slow an thick as treacle.

'So he can smell things of course,' Fergus replies.

'Smell? What can he smell?' Beetle sneers at me.

'Anything,' Fergus says.

Beetle looks down at me; he towers over me by a foot or so an his arms an legs are as thick as tree trunks. His face is round an white like the moon with small dark eyes an fat blubbery lips.

'Anything?' he asks me, menace in his face.

'Aye,' I say, tryin not to let me knees tremble.

Beetle snatches up a jar from the shelf an thrusts it in me face. 'Go on then. What's in that?'

I twist the lid off an hold the jar up to me nose.

The stink of rotten fish guts an sheep fat slaps me in the face an I turn green an retch.

'What is it then, big nose?' Beetle has his thick arms crossed in front of him.

'Fish guts an sheep fat,' I tell him, chokin back the sick an twistin the lid back on sharpish.

'No it aint, you numpty. That there's the finest sea dragon milk.' He snatches the jar back off me. 'I bought it off a peddler for twelve sovs to heal the ulcer on my foot.'

'Then yer a fool,' I tell him, still feelin queasy.

Beetle's hands snatch up the front of me tunic an lift me into the air.

'What did you call me?' he hisses, his furious face only inches from mine. 'You call me a fool when you don't know the difference between fish guts and sea dragon milk?'

I can see Fergus jumpin up an down behind him, panic all over his face an I wonder how close I am to gettin thumped.

'I know the difference between a real herbalist an a scammer!' I tell him.

'You're sayin that vernacular tricked me?' His grip gets even tighter an I'm strugglin fer breath.

'I'm sayin that it'd be near impossible fer anyone to milk a flamin sea dragon!' I choke out.

I can almost see the cogs turnin in his brain while he figures out what I mean an slowly the frown disappears from his face. Those flabby lips turn up in a smile an then a laugh an I see his gummy mouth with only a few black teeth still in it. Beetle puts me down, slaps me on the back hard enough to bruise an keeps on laughin.

'I think he likes you,' Fergus whispers.

'Oh. Good.' I wait fer me heart to stop thunderin in me chest.

Beetle stops laughin at last an offers us a cup of tea.

He might like me but I feel sorry fer the peddler when Beetle catches up with him.

# Finding Pancakes!

by

## MARCIA WILLIAMS

Winifred had been waiting for this day since the moment she hatched. It was the day the yearling monsters found their human child – that special companion they would share their lives with. From the time they broke free of their eggs they had been practising their monstrous skills ready for this day – and none more than little Winifred.

Now the eager monsters all jostled to show off their fiercest profile, sharpest fang, scariest sneer and loudest roar to the audience of excited children. Winifred blew her best smoke rings, flashed rainbow colours through her scales and fast-flapped her wings. In spite of her efforts, Winifred soon found herself pushed behind her larger companions where she quickly became invisible. She tried, and failed, to squash the tears back into her eyes and stop her scales turning grey with disappointment.

Her friends were already walking off, hand in claw, with their new human companions – only Winifred and Nanny Zozo were left in the glade. Nanny Zozo had been overseeing these occasions for years and always felt that there was a special magic that matched each of her monsters to its perfect child, so she wasn't expecting to find a sad little monster left behind.

'Now, now,' she admonished. 'What are you doing here? Don't you want to belong to a human child?'

'Nobody wanted me,' sniffed Winifred.

'Well, maybe that's because you've gone grey and lost your oomph.'

'Grey is my sad colour, and I don't know what "oomph" is.'

'Oomph is the colour in your scales and the hope in your heart that makes all things possible. Find that hope and you'll find your child,' smiled Nanny Zozo as she vanished in a puff of smoke.

So Winifred started searching for hope up trees and under leaves, but she found nothing. Her daddy would know where to find hope, but Winifred had left home that morning knowing it was her time to go out into the world – she couldn't go back. A large tear rolled down Winifred's cheek as she collapsed in a heap and buried her head in her arms.

'Why are you so sad?' asked a small voice.

'I've no human child,' wailed Winifred, without looking up, 'and I can't find any hope.'

'I don't know about hope, but I'm a human child,' said the child.

'That's not possible,' sighed Winifred, still not looking up. 'They've all gone.'

'All except me! I was late because it was pancakes for breakfast.'

'What's pancakes?' asked Winifred. 'Do monsters like pancakes?'

'Shall we go home and find out?' said the child. 'Dad is the best pancake-maker and Mum is really good at finding things, especially hope.'

'Tell me more about pancakes,' snuffled Winifred, looking up at last and holding out a rainbow-coloured claw.

'Well, you can eat them with lemon and sugar, maple syrup, honey, strawberries, raspberries, chocolate spread, cream …'

'Let's go,' smiled Winifred. 'I am definitely your monster – and pancakes are definitely what monsters call hope!'

# FIRSTS

# The First Tear

by

## KEVIN CROSSLEY-HOLLAND

Thorns and thistles.

Aprons of rough fig leaves chafing their skin. And overhead the angry sun.

Adam and Eve staggered away from the Garden of Eden, weighed down by their own heads and hearts.

When God looked down at them, He could see they understood how wrong they had been to eat an apple from the Tree of the Knowledge of Good and Evil when He had forbidden them to do so. He could see their bitter regret and their grief. And He felt pity for them.

Then God spoke to Adam and Eve:

'Wherever you go in the world, you will find much trouble and sorrow as well as pleasures and joys. You will find greed and unkindness. During your short lives, you will see fighting and refugees because that is how the world is. You will ache with the weight of the world.

'But I created you. In Eden I loved you, and I love you now and always. I will always love you.

'Look now at this little pearl. It is called a tear.

'Adam my son, my daughter Eve, when you feel worn out and unhappy, this little pearl will fall from your eyes. Then you'll brace your backs a little, and your sadness will lighten a little, and you'll comfort each other.'

When Adam and Eve heard God's words, their eyes grew hot, they blinked and their tears welled up, then rolled down their rosy cheeks. They held each other.

And since then, if anyone at all feels weighed down by sadness, their tears will rise and flow from their eyes and they will feel a little lighter and better because of them.

# My First Expedition to the Wilderness

by

## ED CLARKE

We had pitched the tent as far away from civilisation as we'd dared. And it was my mission to spend the night in it alone. I only had myself to blame, because I had suggested it. I'd wanted to prove I had what it took. But as I zipped up the door of the tent and shut out the pitch-black night, I immediately had my regrets. My shelter seemed impossibly flimsy against the elements. The slightest breeze made it sway. What if a storm came to tug it from its mooring? What if spindly fingers of lightning found their way to the tent poles?

I steadied my nerves and climbed into my sleeping bag, pulling it all the way up to my chin. It felt safer that way. I stared up at the faint shadows cast across my billowy cotton ceiling. *Vegetation of some kind*, I thought. Or rather, I hoped. I had seen bushes outside before I'd got in but … A rustle! Just outside the tent! A creature! Or creatures?

Could it be bears? Did bears live here? I took a deep breath to calm myself. No, the noise wasn't loud enough for bears. And it would be more snuffly. Perhaps it was a fox on the prowl. Could foxes get into tents? I stared at my zipped door. It seemed secure. It would hold … wouldn't it?

And it was cold. Colder than I thought it would be. I should have brought more clothes. It was too far to go back now. I tried to stop myself from shivering by curling up into a ball.

Somewhere in the darkness a bird sang. And then another. *The birds will keep watch over me*, I thought. The company of the birds would mean I wasn't alone.

Another rustle outside. I was calmer now. It was probably just a mouse. A tiny mother mouse, out searching for food for its children.

Then I imagined all the creatures outside. Great and small. All with families to care for, sheltering from the weather and waiting for the light of the day to come. We were all together, out here in the dark wilderness.

'I've got a hot chocolate out here for you, poppet,' came a voice from outside the tent.

I wriggled over to the door and unzipped it. I thrust out my hand to take the steaming mug from my dad.

'I'm a bit old to be called poppet now, Dad,' I replied.

'Sorry, poppet. Are you sure you're going to be OK out here?'

'Yep. No problem.'

'Good for you. Night, night.'

The hot drink warmed my insides as I watched my dad pad back to the house in his slippers. I zipped the tent back up and settled back down. The wilderness was my back garden again and the night, my friend.

# BELIEVING HARD IN YOURSELF

# An extract from
# *Everdark*

by

## ABI ELPHINSTONE

*In* Everdark, *the prequel to my Unmapped Chronicles series, an eleven-year-old girl called Smudge and a grumpy monkey called Bartholomew set sail across a magical kingdom in an enchanted boat. The extract below opens shortly after a violent storm which Smudge and Bartholomew survive, but now their boat is sinking … I wanted to include this extract because it shows how sometimes the truly extraordinary people in our world – the ones who defeat monsters, save kingdoms and right sinking ships – are simply the ones who believe, full tilt, in themselves, in magic and in hope against all odds.*

The noise of the storm grew quieter as the boat sank further into the depths of the ocean, but Bartholomew's words were loud and clear. 'I might have doubted you at first, Smudge, but I should have had more faith. Most people spend their whole life never knowing the strength that lies inside them. They live timidly and are too scared to speak up or step out. But you are not afraid. You dared to believe that you are capable of extraordinary, impossible things.'

A tear rolled down Smudge's cheek. 'But I was wrong, wasn't I? We're still sinking!'

The boat groaned under the weight of the sea.

Bartholomew squeezed Smudge's hands. It was only a little squeeze but there was something about the way the monkey held her hands, his old paws wrapped firmly round her fingers. Smudge had never thought Bartholomew liked her, but as she looked into the monkey's eyes now she realised, for the first time, that they were big and kind and shining with loyalty.

'It isn't easy to believe in oneself,' Bartholomew said. 'In fact, sometimes it's easier to believe in things like dragons and witches though they are rarely seen. But to know the quiet strength of your spirit – and to count on it in times like these – is to understand what it means to be truly brave.'

Smudge brushed the tears from her eyes.

'I underestimated you,' Bartholomew said, 'but I will never do so again. Because the strength inside you is iron-strong and, if you can find it again now, and hold it, just for a second, I believe things might turn out all right.'

Smudge watched the sea scroll past the cubbyhole window – down, down, down they went – but Bartholomew's words kindled something inside her. She took a long, deep breath and dared to believe in herself again. And, as she did so, a peculiar thing happened ...

The boat stopped sinking and began, very slowly, to drift upwards.

'What's – what's happening?' Smudge gasped.

Bartholomew smiled. 'You filled the lifebuoy attached to this boat with a sea-dragon's breath because you remembered that it's more powerful and more buoyant than ordinary air. But you forgot one thing.' The boat floated on up. 'A sea-dragon's magic only works if the person in charge of it believes in themself as well as in the magic.'

Smudge hugged Bartholomew tight. 'Oh, clever old you for remembering! For telling me to hope!'

The monkey stiffened in her embrace and things became terribly awkward. 'Ahem, yes, very nice. Thank you.' He stood up and shook the water from his fur as the boat bounced up on to the surface of the waves. Then he turned a very serious face towards Smudge. 'If you breathe a word about that hug or my overly sentimental words earlier, I am afraid I shall have to disown you completely. I appear to have lost control of my emotions.' He picked up his trilby and put it on. 'And that will not do at all.'

# Me

by
## SWAPNA HADDOW

I love me.

I love the way I shoot through the sky when I jump, jump,
   JUMP.

I love my stretchy arms and all the shapes I can make.

I love my wobbly belly and my wiggly toes.

I love my curly hair and my brown skin.

I love my brain,

my brilliant thinky brain that maps my voyages and paints my
   daydreams.

But sometimes there are days when I'm not sure I love me as much
   as the day before.

So on those days

I squeeze my eyes shut.
I take a deep breath in.
And I blow that thought away,

                              away.


                                                  So far away.


And I hug my arms around me and squish me hard.

Then
I jump and I stretch and I leap up high.
And I sing and I shout and make shapes and I wiggle my toes and
    wobble my belly
and I dance on my head and think all my thinks.
And I remember just how much
I LOVE BEING ME.

There's a Hero Inside All of Us
by Laura Ellen Anderson

# BIRTHDAYS

# The Flyaway Kite

by
## CATHERINE DOYLE

The kite arrived on Tuesday evening, but it was only a string then. It sat patiently on the doorstep, waiting for the Fitzpatrick family to finish singing 'Happy Birthday'. Oscar, who was in the middle of turning seven years old, was thinking of his wish.

'Hurry,' said his sister, Zoe. 'The candles are melting into the chocolate.'

Oscar blew them out, just as the doorbell rang.

'That was quick!' He slid down the hallway in his socks and swung the front door open. 'I knew you'd – *oh.*'

It was only a small brown box. Inside, Oscar found a spool of silver thread wrapped in a diagram for a simple, homemade kite. And, on the back, a note scrawled in spidery ink:

*Meet me on the moon.*

'I bet it's from Nan,' said Oscar excitedly. 'We always do fun things on my birthday. Like playing frisbee in the park and going shopping for silly costumes …' He trailed off.

'That was before,' said Zoe gently.

Before Nan's house got too big for her. Before the stove got too hot and the stairs too steep. Suddenly, there had been so much cleaning and cooking and remembering to do, they had decided, as a family, that Nan would go somewhere where other people could look after all that stuff. Where they could look after her.

Oscar pretended not to hear his sister. 'Step one,' he said, spreading the diagram between them like a treasure map. 'Sticks.'

Zoe took off to wrestle the tree in their garden. When she came back, Oscar glued two branches together to make a cross.

'Step two: cloth.' Oscar glanced around for their mum, then cut a square out of the tablecloth.

Zoe gasped.

'Quick,' hissed Oscar. 'On to step three.'

The string was the trickiest part. There was a lot of looping and knotting and threading.

Finally, Oscar set the kite down. 'Ready.'

'Wait!' Zoe stuck a pair of googly eyes to it. '*Now* it's ready.'

In the back garden, they grabbed hold of the string as the kite took off in a sudden gust.

They were tugged up, up, up, over the roof and across the neighbourhood. They erupted in giggles as the streets turned to fields and the fields to forest, the countryside unfurling below them like a magnificent green carpet. The wind whooshed them onwards, through misty rain and marshmallow clouds.

And still they flew, until the world shrunk to a blue marble.

The moon rose, big and silver-bright, as the universe threw its arms round them.

The kite kept them aloft, as the stars twinkled hello. 'Room for one more explorer?' A frilly pink kite drifted past them, wearing a matching pair of googly eyes. Nan floated from its silver string, grinning from ear to ear. There was a diamond-shaped hole in the back of her dressing gown.

Oscar's heart did a somersault. 'Nan, you came!'

'You didn't think I'd miss my grandson's birthday, did you?' She winked. 'Not for all the world.'

# The Best Feeling Ever

by
## FLEUR HITCHCOCK

with illustration by
## R.S. McKAY

It's my birthday tomorrow. I'm sitting on my bed with my eyes closed trying to send telepathic messages to my mum.

I'm really hoping that my present will be a pony.

I have dropped all the hints. Galloped over broom handles, made a cardboard saddle and hung it over the banisters. I whinny. I paw the ground. I even say 'Yum' when I eat raw carrots. I've been very consistent with this – I've done it for two years. Last birthday I was given a plastic telescope and a sweater. I managed to hide my disappointment, but this time – this time – maybe I am going to be lucky.

I scrunch my eyes tight and try to visualise the pony. It can be any real pony colour. I don't honestly care. Holding my breath, I try to send a pony picture from my head to Mum's.

Thing is, we've moved house and there's a field at the back of our garden. It's not our field, but it has grass and a shed. Sometimes it's lived in by an old sheep, but the sheep has disappeared. The field has been empty for a whole week.

Maybe it's waiting for a pony, too.

I pull the duvet up around my shoulders and think of horse names until I fall asleep dreaming of wild gallops over the countryside.

In the morning, I wake up before Mum and sit at the top of the stairs, waiting. She must hear me because she comes out of her room and gives me a wink. *Is that a pony wink?* I wonder.

'I've a surprise for you,' she says. 'It's outside.'

I almost explode. I was right. She got the hint. It's going to be a pony.

She's at the door, smiling. 'Ready?' she asks, opening the door.

For a moment I stand, the smile jammed on my stupid face as I stare at a red bicycle which is not, and was never at any point in its life, a pony.

'Wonderful,' I say. 'A bike. How – brilliant.' And I hold the smile on my face and keep the tears out of my eyes.

'Darling,' says Mum, hugging me. 'I knew you'd love it. Have a ride after breakfast.'

I eat cereal, stirring it round and round, blinking back the tears, and then I go out and sit on my new red bicycle. I roll it back and forth along the fence and, because it glides so smoothly, I let it freewheel down the slope to the road. We pick up speed and the bike slicks along the tarmac. I notice that I can see over the hedges, that the wind is catching in my hair. My steed turns downhill again and, in a second, we're galloping over the ground, shooting past potholes, whizzing under branches.

Happiness fizzes up through my chest and I pedal as fast as I can until I can't breathe any more.

'Yes!' I shout. 'Yes, yes! *This* is the best feeling ever!'

305

# REMARKABLE
# FRIENDSHIPS

# Yasmin and Sila

by
## MARIANNE LEVY

Sila liked running and climbing and examining the grazes on her knees. Which was why, when the people came to her village, she did not like the look of Yasmin. Although she had been walking for many miles, Yasmin was perfectly neat and noticeably tidy. Unlike Sila.

It had been a four-scab day and Sila was tired. And now she had to share her bed with someone who tossed and turned.

'Try remembering something nice,' said Sila. 'That's what I do when I can't sleep.' Then, when Yasmin went quiet, she couldn't help but ask, 'What are you thinking of?'

'Sitting in a cafe and drinking tea in the sun.'

'But tea is so hot and slow,' said Sila.

'Iced coffee, then. But only if I can have it with sugar.'

'Five lumps is best,' said Sila.

Yasmin's smile shone through the dark.

And, as they talked, it seemed to Sila that Yasmin's words built a whole city, stone by stone; palm trees and minarets and shining squares. 'The swimming pool, Sila. It's enormous. You should see it!'

'We go swimming,' said Sila. 'I'll take you to the river tomorrow. It's better than any pool. We swim with fish.' *And snakes*, she thought, but decided not to say.

'I would like that,' said Yasmin. And Sila realised that she would like it, too.

Only, when she woke, Yasmin had gone.

It was then that Sila knew she would never see Yasmin again. And that she would never stop looking, even when she found grey in her hair and her climbing days were done.

Sila was sitting in a sunny cafe. She told herself she was resting her legs, which hurt more with every winter that passed, but really she was watching, as she always did, in case she saw a woman with noticeably neat clothes, drinking iced coffee.

Like the woman who had taken the seat at her side.

One lump, two lumps. Three, four. Five.

Hope is a dragon. It can sleep for thirty years. But give it a poke and it will roar.

Which was why Sila's voice shook when she said, 'During the war … there were refugees … and a family stayed in our house. It was just one night. And I—'

But the woman had put down her cup and walked away. How stupid, to think that Yasmin would remember! Or maybe this wasn't Yasmin at all. Perhaps there no longer was a Yasmin. So many people never made it back to this smart new city, its bullet holes hidden behind metal and glass.

Only, then the woman returned leading a little girl with scruffy clothes and messy hair whose knees were scabbing up nicely.

'I'm sorry,' said the woman. 'But there's someone I wanted you to meet. This,' she said, addressing the girl, 'is a dear friend of mine. And this young lady –' and now she looked up and smiled. 'This is my daughter, Sila.'

# Gimme Five

by
## SARAH MASSINI

… with Elsie Nevett and Lilia Moat, both aged 5, giving a helping hand.

This little piggy went walking.
This little piggy stayed at home.
This little piggy had high hopes.
This little piggy baked buns.
And this little piggy …
thought about how …
the first little piggy loved everything that flittered and flowered.

And how the second little piggy knew loads of clever stuff, and could tell a great story too.

And the way the third little piggy pondered over all things bright and beautiful.

And how there'd always be scrummy buns to eat with the fourth piggy around.

And the fifth little piggy could see … how each little piggy knew about SOMETHING, and how together …
TOGETHER …
everything is possible.

And this little piggy called to the other little piggies, 'WE WE WE WE got this!' he cried.

And he jigged and jogged and jumped all the way home.

# The Hideout

by

## ROSS MacKENZIE

'You're going to chicken out.'

Mila shot her big brother a venomous look. 'I am *not* going to chicken out.'

'Yeah? Then what's the hold-up?'

She surveyed the garden, a thick jungle of grass and thorns, and wished she was back in her old house. Back *home*.

'A dare's a dare, Mila.' Either you go inside the haunted shed, or you do my chores for a week.'

'I *know*. I'm *going*.'

Mila buttoned her mac and set off all alone. Her heart raced as she pushed between wet stalks of grass. Along the way she discovered a small pond, some giant rhubarb and an empty bird's nest. Then, at last, she entered the deep shade beneath the chestnut trees, kicked away a wall of nettles and stood before the haunted shed.

All was silent and still.

Gathering her bravery, Mila clutched the handle and opened the creaking door.

The workshop was dark and cobwebbed and smelt of damp.

Long-forgotten pots of paint lay scattered on the filthy floor.

And there, in the corner, sat a scruffy boy.

He had a book on his lap.

Mila blinked. 'What're you doing?'

The boy looked up from his book. 'What's it look like? Shut the door, will you? I'm at a good bit.'

Mila hesitated. 'You're not a ghost … are you?'

He snorted. 'Course not.'

Mila folded her arms. 'You're not supposed to be here.'

'Who're you? The reading police?'

'Nope. This is my garden. Just moved house.'

The boy's eyes grew wide. 'Oh. Please don't tell!'

'What are you reading?'

'Um. *The Witches*.'

'That's a good one! Have you got to the bit with—'

'Don't spoil it!' A pause. 'What's your name?'

'Mila. What's yours?'

'Gabe.'

'How come you aren't reading at home?'

He shrugged. 'Too noisy. I used to have a great spot near the river, but Ben Foley and his gang nicked it. Are you going to tell?'

Mila considered this. 'Nah. Do you have any more books?'

Gabe reached down and produced a bulging rucksack. 'Just a few.'

'Budge up,' said Mila. She sat beside him, picked out *Peter Pan* and began to read.

'I'd better get back.' She offered the book, but Gabe didn't take it.

'Keep it.'

'Really?'

'Yeah. Hey … would you like to be in my reading club?'

'You have a club? Cool. Who else is in it?'

'Just me … so far.' He blushed. 'It's OK if you don't—'

'When d'you want to meet next?' she said.

He looked surprised. And happy. 'Tomorrow? Same time?'

'Deal.'

Mila hummed happily as she chopped back through the garden. How strange it was that she'd set off on a ghost hunt and instead found a friend. Of course, she'd still tell her brother she'd seen a ghost – he wouldn't have the guts to check for himself.

She reached the house, looked back down the garden, and smiled.

Maybe living here wasn't going to be so bad after all.

# My Brother Is a Pangolin

by
## MARIE-ALICE HAREL

We dance and laugh under the stars sometimes,
When days are good and treat us kind.
We hide and cry in tune
When sorrows lay as thick as snow.
He knows secrets I'll never know,
How flowers smile and trees chuckle
As birds fly high above and low.
He tells me so when I listen
It's not his voice, it is the wind,
The secret song of silent things.
With infinite patience they wait,
The wild ones that don't know hate.
If like wings I could spread my arms
and just so, shield them from harm.
My skin, soft and thin,
And his armour of scales,
Both fragile things
Under a high sky ceiling.

He says there's hope in all that grows,
That includes me, and I'm smiling.
His trust is what keeps me going
When days are dark and cold as snow.
My brother is a pangolin,
Because his sorrow is my sorrow.
Ten thousand miles between us count for nothing,
I feel his heart beating, under my skin.

# SMILE

# The Store Full of Magical Things

by
## RUTENDO TAVENGERWEI

I met an old man once
In a store full of magical things
Whistling while he watched me
His crooked hat on his head
'What are you buying, little miss?'
He asked in his cheerful voice
'There is a clock that can send you anywhere
in the world,
An elephant that can fly,
A bar of chocolate that you can never finish …
Or a smile that can never fade.'
So much to choose from
In a store full of magical things,
But once I looked at it,
I knew what I would take home with me,

What I take with me everywhere
What I am sending now to you,
A smile that can never fade
A smile that can never fade.

Fake Smile

by

Jim Smith

# BOOKS

# The Seed

by
## ANDY SHEPHERD

I have a garden. A very small garden that fits on my window sill. Marnie, that's my grandma, turned up one day with a long plastic trough. She barged past Mum and plonked it on my window sill. Then she threw me an envelope and waggled her finger at me. 'Plant them,' she said. And she barged her way out again, leaving me with a wink and the smell of her vanilla hand cream. Mum rolled her eyes and left me to it.

I shook the envelope and heard a gentle shushing sound. Peeling it open and peering in, I found a cluster of tiny seeds. I tipped them out of the packet and rolled them around in my palm. I wondered what they were. Only one way to find out.

I pressed my thumb into the soil in the trough, pinched a seed between finger and muddy thumb and gently dropped it in. Then tucked the soil around it like Mum tucked me into bed. Fifteen little seeds tucked into fifteen little beds.

Moonlight bathed them, sunshine warmed them, tip-tapping rain trickled over them. And I watched and waited.

One day I woke, eyes sticky with sleep, and found a bird scratching at the soil.

'No!' I cried and leaped at the window.

But it was too late. The row of beds lay untucked. Only one seed still safe and snug.

Mum agreed it needed protecting. So I stuck my glove on a wooden spoon and gave it the fiercest painted eyes I could. Then we hung some scrunched-up tin foil from a piece of string so it spun in the wind and glittered.

It grew warm outside, I let my seed drink. I kept watch. And the seed began to grow. Very, very slowly.

Why do things have to grow so slowly?

I had other things to do – I couldn't sit there all day – but I still watched out of the corner of my eye. And whispered to my seed before Mum tucked me in.

Day by day, the tiny shoot grew. Taller and taller. It grew leaves that unfurled like upturned hands, ready to catch the rain. And then one morning I woke to find a bud on the stem.

But really not a bud at all. Because buds are round or pointy and this had corners and leaves of its own. This bud was a book. A tiny, perfect book. Already ripe for the picking. So I did. I picked it like I picked strawberries from the farm we'd visited.

It lay in my hand, whispering back to me. Until I opened it and started to read the tiny words that rushed out and flew me away with them.

Every day I picked another book. And stories bloomed around me.

One day I am going to plant a forest and grow books as far as I can see.

Hope Springs Eternal by Emma Yarlett

# The Magical Thing about Reading

by
## ANNA JAMES

If I was able to bottle up feelings, to keep them safe and release them whenever I wanted, there are a lot that I would try to capture. I would bottle the absolute contentment of eating mince pies and playing board games in front of my grandparents' log fire and the anticipation of something you've been looking forward to for ages. I'd stopper up the sensation that comes from the exhausted satisfaction of climbing to the top of a mountain and the peace and wonder at seeing the world stretched out around you.

A lot of my favourite feelings have something to do with books. On my shelves of bottles you'd find the limitless possibility of walking into a bookshop with a book token in your hand, as well as knowing you've chosen the perfect six-book selection from the library. But one of the most magical feelings for me is the split second you open up a brand new book – and for a moment, whatever book it is, there is the potential that it could be your favourite book in the whole world. I will always be a reader before I'm a writer. Once, before I'd started writing my own books, I mentioned how much I love giving every book I read that moment to be my new favourite, and a friend, who was a writer, told me they thought it was the greatest gift that you could give a book. Now I write my own stories, I understand how true that is.

We never really know which books are going to be our favourites, even if we have authors and types of stories that we know we love. Often, how books look, or what they say on the back, give us clues about what we might expect, but you never quite know when a book is going to feel like it was written just for you. When it's going to make you laugh or cry or think or change just when you need it most. And that's what puts the very real magic into reading.

So that moment of possibility, of excitement, of hope, *that* is my favourite feeling. And the best thing about this feeling is that you can have it whenever or wherever you like by picking up and reading a new book.

# DO IT YOURSELF

# How to Start a Story

by
## JAMES CAMPBELL

Once upon a time. Oh no, hang on. That's a terrible start to a story. No one begins anything with 'Once upon a time' any more. That's literally the worst way to start a story ever. It doesn't even make any sense. How can you be *upon* a time? Are you sitting on a clock? Why would you be sitting on a clock? That wouldn't be very comfortable. Stories also sometimes start with 'Are you sitting comfortably? Then I'll begin.' But you can't be sitting comfortably if you're sitting on a clock.

Maybe it's a really comfortable clock. A bouncy, inflatable Big Ben. Or one of those giant blow-up bananas that people sit on and then get dragged along by a speedboat and they have to hold on really tight, but someone falls off because they weren't concentrating and everyone laughs! You can do your own by sitting a hamster on a real banana. It's difficult though, as their little legs aren't quite long enough to get over the banana. I know. I've tried it with our hamster. It's best to keep bananas and hamsters separate.

It's also best to keep bananas separate from other fruit. They release some sort of gas that makes other fruit go mouldy. Then again, sometimes I release some sort of gas that makes *everything* go mouldy. That's why I have my own special chair. Inside a giant hamster ball.

Male hamsters have to be kept away from other hamsters, as well. Syrian hamsters are fiercely territorial and prefer to be on their own. Maybe it's the same with bananas. They just can't stand other fruit.

But anyway, I'm not starting this story with 'Once upon a time'. Why is it *once* anyway? Can you be *twice* upon a time? Maybe if the story happened two times. Why would that happen? Unless the story was about déjà vu. Déjà vu is what you get when you're doing something and it feels like you've been here before, read this before, said this before, read this before, even though you know for a fact that this is the first time any of this has happened. If this story was about déjà vu then maybe it could start with 'Twice upon a time'.

Or time travel. Maybe the story is about time travel and starts with 'Twice upon a time'. Or 'Three times upon a time'. Or 'Many times upon a time'!

Many times upon a time, I was trapped in a constant loop of space time. Multiple dimensions folded themselves around me like raspberry-ripple ice cream. I fell through time and time fell through me as I surfed up the waterfall of possible universes.

That's an excellent beginning. I could start like that. It's just a shame it doesn't involve bananas. Maybe the banana is a time machine. A time-travelling banana. Yes. That's how I'll start this story.

Here we go then.

Many times upon a time, I rode a multitude of time-travelling bananas. Bananas. Bananas. Bananas. Bananas. Bananas.

# Hunters of Hope

by
## LISSA EVANS

A girl accidentally drops a bar of chocolate down the side of her bed, next to the wall. She heaves the bed to one side and realises that there's a long, low cupboard door behind it and, when she opens the door, she can see a torchlit stone passage leading downward towards an underground river. Floating on the river is a small red rowing boat with her name painted on the side.

A boy buys a horse from a charity shop.

A girl's family adopts a rescue dog. The girl's determined to train it, but it just doesn't seem able to learn commands – not even 'sit' or 'shake hands'. One day, the girl is in her bedroom with the dog when she sees an insect buzzing around.

'Mum,' she shouts. 'There's a fly in here.'

'A what?' calls her mother.

'FLY!' shouts the girl very loudly.

And the dog flies.

A boy receives a letter announcing that a distant great-aunt has died and has left him a very small island in her will. It has a beach, a lake, a hut, a mysterious monument and a flock of wild parrots, but he has to agree to live there for a week on his own before it's legally his.

A girl comes home from school and sees that the road outside her house has been dug up. There's a big hole surrounded by barriers, and out of the hole is climbing a small, lost-looking dinosaur.

A boy lives with his family in a tiny flat. 'We've bought a house!' his parents announce, one day. 'It's huge, but we got it for almost nothing.'

'You'll love it,' his mum says. 'The only thing is, we can't have anything metal indoors.'

'Why not?' asks the boy.

'Because it's next to a factory that makes magnets.

But I'm sure it won't cause us any problems …'

# My Favourite Game

### by
## HARRIET MUNCASTER

The first thing you need to do is find a pocket-sized doll or bear to be your tiny friend. You probably have one lying round your house somewhere. Make sure to give them a name! You could even make them a miniature birth certificate.

Your little character probably needs some clothes. Are there any scraps of fabric you can use to make some? Or maybe your character loves dressing up best. Tin foil would work well to make a robot costume. A strip of ribbon could be made into a tutu skirt!

Your tiny friend will probably want to adventure around your house. Think about how different everything would look if you were only ten centimetres high. A rumpled duvet could be a snowy mountain. Two lolly sticks would make perfect skis.

How about making a miniature explorer's kit? A piece of string for rope, a paper clip for a grappling hook, a stub of pencil and tiny notebook for recording adventures in. Maybe you could even get an adult to help you make a fairy-sized backpack to put it all in.

If you have a garden, your little friend might like to explore out there. The grass would be like a jungle, the flowers like tall umbrellas! Can you find some miniature leaves that you are allowed to pick? You could stick them in your tiny explorer's notebook as 'findings'.

You could even take some photos of your character adventuring. Really get down to their level so you can see what the world looks like through their eyes.

You might like to take your tiny friend on a picnic. Use a small square of fabric for a rug. One fairy cake is the size of a big birthday cake to your character. You could ice it all over and decorate it. Sprinkles make perfect tiny sweets. You could even create real miniature pizzas and sandwiches too! Take one slice of bread and squash or roll it flat. Cut out a small circle, spread it with tomato purée (or ketchup!) and sprinkle with cheese. Cook it for a few minutes and you will have a perfect fairy-sized pizza!

What else can you make for your tiny friend? An ice-cream tub could make a great swimming pool! A bowl of water could become a jacuzzi if you blow bubbles into it with a straw. A margarine tub could be made into a boat to sail across a pond, or in the bath. An upside-down book could be a tent! A cardboard box could be the beginning of a cosy little house for them to live in ...

What tiny adventures will you go on?

# The Incredible Instant Joke-Creating Machine

by
## SUSIE DAY

Here are three facts everyone should know:

1. Laughing at something funny is the very best feeling.
2. Jokes are funny.
3. You only need to know three jokes.

Joke number one:

What do you get if cross a **vampire** with a **snowman**? **Frostbite**.

Joke number two:

What is a **witch**'s favourite subject at school? **Spelling**.

Joke number three:

What do you call a man with a **bird** on his **head**? **Cliff**.

Did you laugh? Only a little bit? Not at all? That's OK – you're going to fix that now.

See the words in **bold**? Pshoom! They're gone. Now you need to feed the Incredible Instant Joke-Creating Machine with some new words and see what comes out. (Your teacher would tell you all those words are nouns, which means they're names for things – those will make the funniest jokes.)

Here are a few spare words to start you off:

Apple

Triple-decker ice-cream sundae

Armpit

Mrs Bottomly-Smith

Goldfish

Terrifying screamy nightmare

Hula hoop

Werewolf

Potato salad

Thumb

Undercrackers

Lionel

Just feed the new words into the Incredible Instant Joke-Creating Machine, turn the handle, twiddle a few dials and flick a few switches (you'll have to do all of this bit in your head) …

What do you get if you cross a **hula hoop** with a **goldfish**?
**Mrs Bottomly-Smith**!

What is a **potato salad**'s favourite subject at school?
**Armpit**!

What do you call a man with **undercrackers** on his **werewolf**?
**Terrifying screamy nightmare!**

Now make your own list of words, and prepare to amaze your friends
and family with your incredible comedic skills!

Colour In! by Liz Pichon

# EXCELLENTLY
# REVOLTING

# Pull My Finger

by

## ANTHONY McGOWAN

'Pull my finger!' said my brother, Kevin, who's just started at big school. He's really, really annoying.

'Get lost!' I said. 'Pull your own finger.'

There was a moment of shocked silence. My baby sister's mouth fell open and some mashed-up Weetabix dribbled out.

I'd broken one of the rules, one of the laws of nature, like, don't walk on the cracks, and never pick the scab from your belly button or all your blood gushes out until you've got none left.

Eventually, my brother said: 'You can't pull your own finger. It doesn't work. It's like trying to lift yourself up by your ears.'

I tried lifting myself up by my ears. That much was right. You can't.

'I don't care. It's gross and I'm late for school.'

'If you don't pull my finger, it will fester inside me and I'll die. Everyone knows that.'

'Too late, I'm out of here.'

'It'll be your fault when I'm dead ...'

*

At school, I told my friend Adil. He shook his head sadly.

'Bad, really bad.'

Then I told Liam.

'No way! If someone says pull, you've got to pull.'

So then I told Louise. 'He may be OK,' she said. 'But then again ...'

It was then that I really started to worry.

I didn't eat any of my lunch. Not just because it was horrid, although it was (broccoli!). All I could think about was my brother, who might already be dead from the fart going bad inside him.

I kept thinking I'd get called in to the Head's office, and she'd look at me with a sad face and tell me what had happened.

When the end-of-day bell went I ran all the way home. As I feared, the doctor was there. He stood in the living room with my mum and dad.

'It's Kevin,' said Mum. 'He's ... he's ...' She couldn't finish. She put her head on my dad's shoulder and sobbed.

The doctor looked at me.

'You're his only hope. Go in to him and see what you can do.'

Kevin lay in bed. His face was the colour of a dead whale. He held out his hand towards me, one finger extended.

The doctor and everyone else had followed me into the bedroom.

I looked at the doctor. He nodded. 'Go ahead.'

I reached out and pulled the trembling finger.

Nothing.

I heard my mother sob again. Sweat began to run down my face.

I tried again, pulling harder. This time the duvet made a small movement, like the surface of a pond ruffled by a slight breeze. But my brother's eyes were still dull.

Last chance. I yanked the finger with all my might. A noise like an enraged elephant fighting a tiger filled the room. The duvet was blown completely off. The windows rattled. A smell of burning underpants filled the room.

'You've done it!' cried my dad.

'You've saved him!' yelled Mum.

'Goo-goo!' said my sister.

So, there you have it.

You've been warned.

If someone says pull my finger, you pull it.

End of story.

# The Indigo Flamingo

by
## NICK LAKE

Once, in a far-off swamp,
There lived a sad little flamingo
Whose name was ... Bob.

Bob was ALMOST exactly what
You would expect from a flamingo,
Named Bob or not.

He had loooooooong legs.
He had feathers.
He had the biggest beak in Mozambique.

But.

You might quite probably think
That Bob, like his pals,
Was a snazzy shade of pink.

If this IS what you think, then no:
Bob was not pink but indigo –
The most indigo flamingo you could ever
wish to know.

That is:

He was a sort of purply-blue.
Blue like the light of the rising moon,
Blue like the blue of the deep lagoon.

And did Bob like it?
Not one bit.
It made him mope and cry,
It made him moan and spit.

I wish, I hope, I wish, he'd think –
That I could not be indigo,
But a beautiful pink.

Oh, the other flamingos were OK.
During the day they'd chat to him,
And sing and dance and play.

But it was once there was no more sun
That being an indigo flamingo
Became not a lot of fun.

See:

When it was dark, Bob BLENDED IN.
His blue wasn't odd then –
It was the colour of EVERYTHING.

*Then* it was like he wasn't there,
Then he was suddenly nothing,
Just part of the midnight air.

The others would talk, right over his head,
They'd trample him, sometimes,
When he went to his bed.

Until one night.

Bob was moping, singing his sad song,
When a great hungry crocodile
Came sneaking along.

Bob was the only one who saw:
The others slept calmly on,
He heard them whistle and snore.

'HEY!' he shouted. 'Hey, Crocodile!
Get your slithery back
And your toothy smile

*OUT*
Of our swamp.
Go on, get lost,
Scarper, be gone!'

The crocodile panicked,
Its eyes bulging out,
It couldn't see anyone,
But it could hear someone shout.

What was this ruckus?
A ghost, or some such?
The croc didn't know,
But he didn't like it much.

He turned on his tail,
Swam fast, swam faster,
With several great splashes
He was gone, he had scarpered.

Now all the other flamingos,
Hearing this loud din,
Woke up and came along,
To see this most amazing thing.

'HOORAY!' they shouted,
Standing in a row.

'Bob, you're our hero!
Thank GOODNESS you're indigo!'

Yes, for once, Bob was happy to be blue.
For once he laughed and smiled,
He danced and capered too.

Until …

Later that night, when Bob was sleeping,
A tired elephant passed by,
And its giant eyes didn't see him.

Then …

Right on the spot where Bob was lying …

The elephant turned itself twice around,
Gave a wide stretch and a great big yawn,
And got ready to flop himself down.
And …

As the elephant sat heavily, and sighed,
Bob disappeared up its fat behind.

And in the morning when the elephant got up
From sitting down –

Bob wasn't indigo any more,
He was a certain shade of brown.

So …

This all goes to show:
You should be very careful what you hope
And what you wish for –
ESPECIALLY if you're indigo.

# TAKING FLIGHT

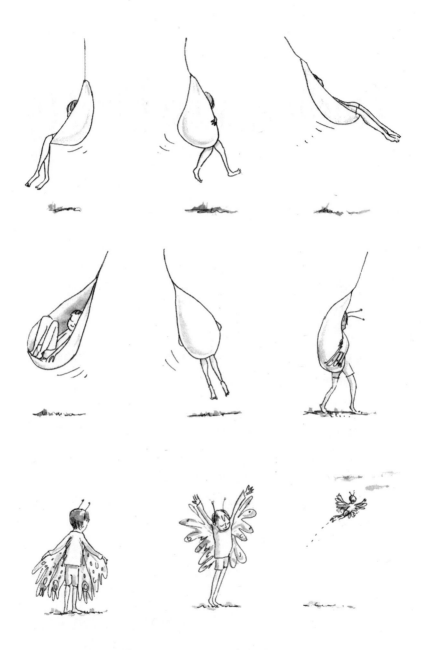

Daydreaming by Polly Dunbar

# Teaching a Bird to Fly

by

## THOMAS TAYLOR

When my brother was old enough he learned to ride a moped. But this story isn't about that, it's about something he brought home one day in his helmet.

'What have you got now?' we said, and my brother held out his helmet like a bowl and replied.

'A bird.'

Inside was a tiny fluffball of brown and yellow, with an open beak.

'*Peep, peep, peep!*' came out of that beak.

'But that's a duckling!' we all said. Sometimes when something is really obvious, people say it out loud anyway. 'What are you doing with a duckling?'

'Found it,' said my brother. 'On the road. Lost. Near the lake, but not near enough.'

'No mother duck will want it back,' we said. 'Not now it smells of you.'

'*Peeep, peeeep!*'

My brother shrugged.

'He's called Dippy.'

Well, Dippy was a goner for sure. No way he could survive, even with a shoebox of shredded paper to hide in. And no matter that my brother took him for walks in the garden – great teenaged feet stumping like a gentle giant's beside the tiny, peeping thing.

'He'll starve,' we said. 'You can't just feed a duck breadcrumbs, you know.'

'I've got it covered,' was all my brother would say to that.

Secretly, he was using my chess game as a chopping board to cut up earwigs, leaving scored diagonals of brown across the black-and-white chequers.

Dippy got bigger and bigger on his earwig diet, following my brother everywhere till his 'peeping' turned to 'quacks'. Eventually, he got so big we could see he wasn't a *he* at all, but a she-duck.

'A mallard, actually,' my brother explained.

'You can't keep a mallard as a pet!' we explained back.

'Why not?'

My brother stroked Dippy where she sat on his lap, in front of the TV.

'Because … a cat will get her. Or a fox. She's still a goner. It's only a matter of time.'

And we were right. In a way.

One day, when my brother rode his moped, Dippy followed him all the way down the lane.

My brother brought her back, but she followed him again – running as fast as a mallard can run, and flapping like mad.

She did this, for *days*.

'I'm teaching her to fly!' My brother would shout, jumping on his moped and zooming off down the lane. And all we could do was shake our heads as he passed back and forth in front of the house, pursued by a duck. Until one day he roared past, hunched over the handlebars, and Dippy was in the air above his head.

Flying!

She lived in the garden after that, until – following my brother around for one last time – she took off and flew away for good.

'She's a goner all right,' my brother said, a week later.

But the next year a pair of mallards came to our garden – a male and a female – and stayed for several days. We never knew for sure but my brother always believed it was Dippy, home again to have ducklings of her own.

And I think he's right.

Bird by Sam Usher

# The Young Bird-Catcher

by

## KATHERINE RUNDELL

It was a year of extravagant fashions: dresses were worn with so many petticoats that it was possible to hide a small dog and two large squirrels under your skirts. Top hats were a full foot high.

Robert had one such top hat. He'd always felt ridiculous in it, but his uncle, who owned the bird shop, insisted. 'If you want to flog expensive nonsense to rich folk,' he said, 'you've got to make them think you're one of them.'

Robert was just nineteen, but that was old enough to know three things. One: every day he went out in the ridiculous hat, tending to the luxury birds bought by the likes of Squire Blenkinsop and Lord Chatterjee, and every day he thought, *We're selling living things for dead money.* Two: no matter how often he went, Elizabeth Chatterjee was never going to look at him, let alone notice how his heart took flight when he saw her. Three: one day he was going to leave town, to study the migration of the swift, and never see a cage again.

That Monday, there was a budgie with bad breath and a parrot who had developed a new and startling vocabulary. The final house was Squire Blenkinsop's. As soon as he stepped inside, Robert knew something was wrong. No house with birds should be so silent.

A maid led him upstairs. 'It's best not to breathe too loud, if you can help it. Blenkinsop likes the world to be seen and not heard. He has the clocks made special, not to tick. In there.'

The room was vast, and lined with bird cages: glorious red and green kingfishers, creamy brown larks, a vivid-bright bluebird. They were all completely still.

'They don't get fed if they sing, or flutter about too much,' said the maid. There was a noise downstairs. 'That'll be the master.' She curtsied out.

Robert acted fast. He threw open the cages, and the window. 'Fly!' he said. But they wouldn't move. Hands shaking, Robert laid the birds in his hat: a dozen, two dozen. They lay still as corpses. He put the hat on, holding it with one hand, and ran into the street.

He needed only to make it to the park. Once he was there, he told himself, he could let them out, and nobody would know.

Then three things happened at once. One: the birds began to wake; there was a fluttering and a scratching against Robert's scalp. Two: there was a sudden roar as Squire Blenkinsop appeared at his door. 'Stop! Bird thief!' he cried, and a policeman came running. And three: around the corner, with her green eyes and generous smile, rode Elizabeth Chatterjee.

His heart began to flutter like the birds.

Hope – mad, tenacious hope, the kind of hope that makes your arms and legs act without your permission – seized hold of Robert. He threw fear to the winds, stepped in front of her horse – 'Miss Chatterjee' – and bowed low.

And he swept off his hat.

A flock of birds erupted into the sky and, for a moment, Elizabeth disappeared inside a cloud of wings. Larks circled around her head, singing for joy.

Elizabeth's eyes, laughing, kingfisher green, met his.

She lifted her skirt; a squirrel's head peeked out.

She held out a hand. There was space behind her for another rider.

'Come,' she said, and he went.

Hope by Chris Haughton

# Further Reading

## PICTURE BOOKS

*We Catch the Bus* by Katie Abey

*I Am Bear* by Ben Bailey Smith and Sav Akyüz

*Sofia Valdez, Future Prez* by Andrea Beaty and David Roberts

*Octopus Shocktopus!* by Peter Bently and Steven Lenton

*Odd Dog Out* by Rob Biddulph

*Mighty Min* by Melissa Castrillón

*Plumdog: Love Is My Favourite Thing* by Emma Chichester Clark

*Hello, Friend!* by Rebecca Cobb

*What the Ladybird Heard at the Seaside* by Julia Donaldson and
   Lydia Monks

*The Smeds and the Smoos* by Julia Donaldson and Axel Scheffler

*There's a Pig Up My Nose!* by John Dougherty and Laura Hughes

*The Pirates of Scurvy Sands* by Jonny Duddle

*Pirate Stew* by Neil Gaiman and Chris Riddell

*Cyril and Pat* by Emily Gravett

*Don't Worry, Little Crab* by Chris Haughton

*The Best Place in the World* by Petr Horáček

*The Girl and the Dinosaur* by Hollie Hughes and Sarah Massini

*Would You Like a Banana?* by Yasmeen Ismail

*The Wildest Cowboy* by Garth Jennings and Sara Ogilvie

*The Haunted Lake* by P.J. Lynch

*While We Can't Hug* by Eoin McLaughlin and Polly Dunbar

*Lubna and Pebble* by Wendy Meddour and Daniel Egnéus

*Mrs Noah's Garden* by Jackie Morris and James Mayhew

*Fly, Tiger, Fly* by Rikin Parekh

*Meesha Makes Friends* by Tom Percival

*I Don't Like Books. Never. Ever. The End.* by Emma Perry and
    Sharon Davey

*Moth: An Evolution Story* by Isabel Thomas and Daniel
    Egnéus

*Seasons* by Sam Usher

*How to Be a Lion* by Ed Vere

*Hiding Heidi* by Fiona Woodcock

*Dragon Post* by Emma Yarlett

## FOR YOUNGER READERS

*Annie Lumsden, the Girl from the Sea* by David Almond, illustrated
    by Beatrice Alemagna

*Amelia Fang and the Naughty Caticorns* by Laura Ellen Anderson

*The Nine Lives of Furry Purry Beancat* by Philip Ardagh, illustrated
    by Rob Biddulph

*The Restless Girls* by Jessie Burton, illustrated by Angela Barrett

*My Headteacher Is a Vampire Rat!* by Pamela Butchart, illustrated
    by Thomas Flintham

*Fairytales Gone Bad: Zombierella* by Joseph Coelho, illustrated
    by Freya Hartas

*Charlie Changes into a Chicken* by Sam Copeland, illustrated
    by Sarah Horne

*Storm* by Kevin Crossley-Holland, illustrated by Alan Marks

*Madame Badobedah* by Sophie Dahl, illustrated by Lauren O'Hara

*Many: The Diversity of Life on Earth* by Nicola Davies, illustrated by
    Emily Sutton

*Dave Pigeon* by Swapna Haddow, illustrated by Sheena Dempsey

*Hortari* by Marie-Alice Harel

*Fabio the World's Greatest Flamingo Detective: Peril at Lizard Lake* by
    Laura James, illustrated by Emily Fox

*Isadora Moon Goes to School* by Harriet Muncaster

*Fantastically Great Women Who Saved the Planet* by Kate Pankhurst

*Witch Wars* by Sibéal Pounder, illustrated by Laura Ellen Anderson

*Pugs of the Frozen North* by Phillip Reeve and Sarah McIntyre

*The Boy Who Grew Dragons* by Andy Shepherd, illustrated
    by Sara Ogilvie

*Claude at the Palace* by Alex T. Smith

*A Super Weird! Mystery: Danger at Donut Diner* by Jim Smith

## FOR OLDER READERS

*The Infinite* by Patience Agbabi

*The Girl Who Speaks Bear* by Sophie Anderson, illustrated
    by Kathrin Honesta

*Piglettes* by Clémentine Beauvais

*Asha & the Spirit Bird* by Jasbinder Bilan

*Corey's Rock* by Sita Brahmachari, illustrated by Jane Ray

*When Secrets Set Sail* by Sita Brahmachari

*Cogheart* by Peter Bunzl

*The Dragon with a Chocolate Heart* by Stephanie Burgis

*The Ice Bear Miracle* by Cerrie Burnell

*Moonchild: Voyage of the Lost and Found* by Aisha Bushby, illustrated
by Rachael Dean

*The Funny Life of Sharks* by James Campbell, illustrated by Rob Jones

*Clarice Bean Spells Trouble* by Lauren Child

*The Secret Dragon* by Ed Clarke

*Jelly* by Jo Cotterill

*Runaway Robot* by Frank Cottrell-Boyce, illustrated by Steven Lenton

*The Great Elephant Chase* by Gillian Cross

*Max Kowalski Didn't Mean It* by Susie Day

*The Storm Keeper's Island* by Catherine Doyle

*The Good Hawk* by Joseph Elliott

*Rumblestar* by Abi Elphinstone

*Wed Wabbit* by Lissa Evans

*Who Let the Gods Out?* by Maz Evans

*The Girl Who Stole an Elephant* by Nizrana Farook

*The Lost Soul Atlas* by Zana Fraillon

*Invisible in a Bright Light* by Sally Gardner

*The Maker of Monsters* by Lorraine Gregory

*Wildspark* by Vashti Hardy

*The Afterwards* by A.F. Harrold, illustrated by Emily Gravett

*Clifftoppers: The Arrowhead Moor Adventure* by Fleur Hitchcock

*Alex Rider: Nightshade* by Anthony Horowitz

*Fly Me Home* by Polly Ho-Yen

*The Iron Man* by Ted Hughes and Chris Mould

*High-Rise Mystery* by Sharna Jackson

*Pages & Co.: Tilly and the Bookwanderers* by Anna James, illustrated
by Paola Escobar

*Kid Normal* by Greg James and Chris Smith, illustrated
by Erica Salcedo

*Queen of Freedom: Defending Jamaica* by Catherine Johnson

*The Strangeworlds Travel Agency* by L.D. Lapinski

*The Beetle Collector's Handbook* by M. G. Leonard, illustrated
by Carim Nahaboo

*Accidental Superstar* by Marianne Levy

*Dare to be Different* by Geraldine McCaughrean, Malorie
Blackman et al.

*The Donut Diaries of Dermot Milligan* by Anthony McGowan,
illustrated by David Tazzyman

*The Time of Green Magic* by Hilary McKay

*Evernight* by Ross MacKenzie

*The Land of Roar* by Jenny McLachlan, illustrated by Ben Mantle

*Goodnight Mister Tom* by Michelle Magorian

*The Girl of Ink & Stars* by Kiran Millwood Hargrave

*The Midnight Guardians* by Ross Montgomery

*The Puffin Keeper* by Michael Morpurgo, illustrated by Benji Davies

*A Chase in Time* by Sally Nicholls, illustrated by Rachael
Dean

*My Headteacher Is an Evil Genius* by Jack Noel

*Wolf Brother* by Michelle Paver

*Shoe Wars* by Liz Pichon

*The Night Bus Hero* by Onjali Q. Raúf

*The Good Thieves* by Katherine Rundell

*Varjak Paw* by SF Said, illustrated by Dave McKean

*The Snow Angel* by Lauren St John, illustrated by Catherine Hyde

*Bloom* by Nicola Skinner, illustrated by Flavia Sorrentino

*My Cousin Is a Time Traveller* by David Solomons

*Murder Most Unladylike* by Robin Stevens

*The Monster in the Lake* by Louie Stowell, illustrated by Davide Ortu

*Circus of Thieves and the Raffle of Doom* by William Sutcliffe,
    illustrated by David Tazzyman

*Malamander* by Thomas Taylor

*The Boy Who Fooled the World* by Lisa Thompson

*The Last Wild* by Piers Torday

*Nevermoor: The Trials of Morrigan Crow* by Jessica Townsend

*Dragon Mountain* by Katie and Kevin Tsang

*Hamish and the Baby Boom!* by Danny Wallace, illustrated by Jamie
    Littler

*Cane Warriors* by Alex Wheatle

*Cloud Boy* by Marcia Williams

*The Orphans of St Halibut's* by Sophie Wills, illustrated
    by David Tazzyman

*Hetty Feather* by Jacqueline Wilson, illustrated by Nick Sharratt

*Taylor & Rose Secret Agents: Peril in Paris* by Katherine Woodfine,
    illustrated by Karl James Mountford

## YOUNG ADULT

*Toffee* by Sarah Crossan

*The Curious Incident of the Dog in the Night-Time* by Mark Haddon

*Nowhere on Earth* by Nick Lake

*Burn* by Patrick Ness

*My Sister Lives on the Mantelpiece* by Annabel Pitcher

*The Monstrous Child* by Francesca Simon

*The Colours That Blind* by Rutendo Tavengerwei

BLOOMSBURY CHILDREN'S BOOKS
Bloomsbury Publishing Plc
50 Bedford Square, London WC1B 3DP, UK
29 Earlsfort Terrace, Dublin 2, Ireland

BLOOMSBURY, BLOOMSBURY CHILDREN'S BOOKS and the
Diana logo are trademarks of Bloomsbury Publishing Plc

First published in Great Britain in 2020 by Bloomsbury Publishing Plc
This edition published in Great Britain in 2020
by Bloomsbury Publishing Plc

3

Typeset by Westchester Publishing Services

Printed and bound in Great Britain by CPI Group (UK) Ltd, Croydon CR0 4YY

To find out more about our authors and books visit www.bloomsbury.com
and sign up for our newsletters

# Acknowledgements

'Mr Umbo's Umbrellas', copyright © Patience Agbabi 2017, commissioned by and first heard on BBC Radio 4; 'A Way to the Stars', copyright © David Almond 2020; 'The Hummingbird's Smile', copyright © Sophie Anderson 2020; 'Look Out: A Poem of Hope', copyright © Philip Ardagh 2020; 'A New Sun-Up', copyright © Ben Bailey Smith 2020; 'Sick Leave', copyright © Clémentine Beauvais 2020; 'The Lamagaia Nest', copyright © Jasbinder Bilan 2020; 'The Gift of Time', text copyright © Sita Brahmachari 2020; 'Football Boots', copyright © Peter Bunzl 2020; 'Spells for Home', copyright © Stephanie Burgis Samphire 2020; 'Stronger Than Magic', copyright © Cerrie Burnell 2020; 'Daphne and the Doughnuts', copyright © Peebo & Pilgrim Ltd 2020; 'Jeddi's Attic', copyright © Aisha Bushby 2020; 'The Toilet Ghost Dog!', copyright © Pamela Butchart 2020; 'How to Start a Story', copyright © James Campbell 2020; 'My First Expedition to the Wilderness', copyright © Ed Clarke 2020; 'Hope Hunter', copyright © Joseph Coelho 2020; 'The Hope Machine', copyright © Sam Copeland 2020; 'Butterfly Field' and 'Waterfall', copyright © Jo Cotterill 2020; 'Murkaster', copyright © Frank Cottrell-Boyce 2020; 'A Box of Pencils', copyright © Gillian Cross 2020; 'Vince', copyright © Sarah Crossan 2020; 'The First Tear', copyright © Kevin Crossley-Holland 2020; 'Hope Is an Ancient Reptile', copyright © Sophie Dahl 2020; 'Lockdown Cat Haircut', copyright © Sharon Davey 2020; 'The Incredible Instant Joke-Creating Machine', copyright © Susie Day 2020; 'The Flyaway Kite', copyright © Catherine Doyle 2020; 'A-Viking in the Springtime', copyright © Jonny Duddle 2020; 'Bag for Life', copyright © Joseph Elliott 2020; Extract

## ILLUSTRATIONS